ROMANCE

W9-BYQ-379

Large Print Ken
Kendrick, Sharon.
Seduced by the boss

FEB   2001

GAYLORD M

SEDUCED
BY THE BOSS

SEDUCED
BY THE BOSS

BY

SHARON KENDRICK

MILLS & BOON®

Special thanks to computer whizz-kid Paul Shreve,
the beautiful wordsmith, Meg,
and their three amazing children, Kate, Mark and Nate.

*First published in Great Britain 2000
Large Print edition 2000
Harlequin Mills & Boon Limited,
Eton House, 18-24 Paradise Road,
Richmond, Surrey TW9 1SR*

© Sharon Kendrick 2000

ISBN 0 263 16729 1

*Set in Times Roman 17 on 17½ pt.
16-1200-48055*

*Printed and bound in Great Britain
by Antony Rowe Ltd, Chippenham, Wiltshire*

CHAPTER ONE

IT STARTED with a letter.

Megan weighed it in her hand and studied it. A love letter, she thought.

The envelope was pink and had the fat, pampered feel of something which had been taken care of—and the handwriting was careful—using proper ink from a proper pen.

She turned the envelope over and smiled. How absolutely wonderful—to think that her coolly demanding boss was the recipient of yet another of these extravagant envelopes!

Who'd have thought it? Mr Cool getting love letters! Why, it almost made him seem human!

Except that Mr Cool hadn't been living up to his name just lately. He had been edgy. Irritable. Uptight.

She just didn't know why.

Megan had been working for Dan McKnight at Softshare for nearly three months now—and she still kept having to pinch herself. The offices were buzzy, the

5

staff were young and it was almost obscenely well paid.

No, jobs in the computer industry of this calibre didn't exactly grow on trees and Megan counted her blessings each and every day. And okay—maybe some women *did* look down their nose when you told them you were a personal assistant—especially to a *man*—but that was their problem, not hers!

Softshare was American-owned and cutting edge, its aim unashamed domination of the software market. A forward-thinking, right-on company—where the workforce was ninety per cent men to ten per cent women.

Which in theory should have been a single girl's dream. The only trouble was that most of the men looked pretty much the same. And the way they looked was nothing to get excited about.

Only one stood apart from the rest of the herd—and that was Dan McKnight. Because Megan's boss was the man who not only didn't fit the technological stereotype—he had taken the mould and broken it into a thousand pieces!

As an industry famous for its lack of pretension and rules, the computer world attracted its fair share of nerds and boffins. But Dan was different. The nerds favoured pony-tails but Dan visited a barber shop regularly, and somehow he timed it so that his hair was never too long and never too short.

Most people in the building wore jeans and T-shirts and sometimes even kicked their shoes off when they were sitting at their desk. But not Dan. With his unruffled hair and per-fect grey suits, Dan always looked as cool and as uncreased as if he had just stepped from the pages of a brand-new magazine.

Such a pity she didn't find him attractive!

Megan turned the letter over in her hand and frowned as the door of the office was flung open and in walked Dan McKnight himself. She sat up immediately, the way she used to do at school when the headmaster came into the classroom unannounced.

And, when she came to think of it, wasn't there something about him which reminded her of a head teacher? A kind of steely de-termination which meant that he usually got what he wanted without appearing to want it at all!

He was exceptionally tall—with both the height and the body to make the most of a suit. He always wore suits—cool grey suits which matched his eyes and contrasted with that neatly cut dark hair.

Only his mouth seemed at odds with the quietly controlled character of the man. It was too lush, too Latin—and far too sensual to belong to Dan McKnight, Megan had decided!

'So what's he *like*?'

Megan's housemate was always asking her this particular question and Megan always had difficulty answering it. Because Dan had such a cool, analytical way of looking at people that it was hard to know what actually made him tick—though it certainly wasn't for want of trying!

She knew that he was single and lived in an exclusive London suburb and had one of the keenest minds in the computer industry. But that was about all she'd gathered, other than his glaringly obvious attributes of being too rich and too smart and too handsome. And much too bad-tempered.

'Good morning Dan,' she said politely.

Dan had been deep in thought and her words shattered his concentration. He screwed his eyes up at her as if trying to remember who she was, then gave a small smile of satisfaction as he shut the office door behind him.

His new assistant seemed to be shaping up just fine, he thought. Hard-working. Enthusiastic. She was easy on the eye, too— though maybe not in the conventional sense. His eyes narrowed and he allowed a reluctant smile to cross his lips. She obviously had no vanities.

Today was a perfect example. That plain pair of beige trousers and an indeterminate-looking cream sweater did nothing for her rather sallow complexion, he decided. Dan liked his assistants to be ultra-efficient—and Megan was efficient, no question about that. He just didn't like them to look too decorative—and so Megan fitted the bill perfectly.

Some of the other directors at Softshare had made the mistake of hiring secretaries who looked like out-of-work actresses. And Dan had watched with a kind of wry amusement as those same directors had struggled to keep their minds on the job instead of on a magnificent pair of legs!

'Good morning, Megan,' he said as he put his briefcase down.

'How was the play last night?' she queried.

Dan knitted his brows together. Had he *told* her he was going to the theatre? 'It was...competent.'

'I'm sure the playwright would be flattered to hear such a glowing description,' observed Megan, with a sunny smile. 'I saw it myself last week—and I thought it was *terrific*!'

'Really? What a remarkable coincidence.' He gave her a chilly look which matched his uninterested tone and stifled a sigh. If there was one thing he could fault Megan Phillips on, it was her irrepressible need to *chatter*. She talked about anything and everything. All the time. She wanted his views on music and newspapers and the state of the economy.

And sometimes—to his horror—he actually found himself discussing these things with her!

Dan frowned. 'Perhaps we could get down to some work now—that is, if we've got all the theatre reviews out of the way?'

Which Megan supposed meant that she should shut up. Trouble was that she had trouble shutting up—which came from growing up in a large, noisy family, she supposed.

'Shall I make us some coffee first?' she asked eagerly.

His look was repressive. 'Not for me—I've only just eaten breakfast.'

'Oh. Right. Well, look what arrived in the post this morning.' She held the plump pink envelope aloft.

'Mmm?' he said absently.

'A letter.'

He paused in the act of hanging his jacket up and gave it a flicker of a glance, but she saw his features tighten. 'Yes, I can see what it is!'

'Another one,' she emphasised deliberately.

'Just put it in my tray, would you?'

Megan felt a stab of concern. Someone had clearly gone to a lot of trouble with this letter—surely he owed it more than that rather dismissive glance? 'Aren't you going to read it?'

Dan turned around, irritation sparking the dark grey eyes. She sounded just like his mother! 'I *beg* your pardon?'

'Well, it's just that I noticed several other envelopes which looked like this—'

'And?' he snapped.

'And you haven't even bothered to read them,' she finished.

'Oh, no—' Dan shook his head and glowered. 'To say that I haven't "bothered" to read them implies that I've been either careless or neglectful. I chose *not* to read them.'

Megan's curiosity was stirred, wondering who in their right mind could resist a handwritten envelope. 'May I ask why?'

She was treated to an impatient glance.

'No, you may not ask why! You're paid to assist me—not interrogate me! So refresh my mind by telling me what's on the agenda for this morning, will you, Megan? And put the letter in my tray like I asked you to. There's a good girl.'

The patronising term annoyed her, but she didn't show it. Reminding herself that the salary Softshare paid her was worth withstanding the occasional moody outburst, Megan gritted her teeth behind her most patient smile. 'Certainly. There were two messages on your voice mail from Japan. Oh, and another call from the Czech Republic. Someone in the government there needs to talk to you and wondered if you could get back to them as soon as possible?'

'Yep. Sure.' He wandered over to the window and looked down onto the car park where a dozen powerful cars, including his own, glittered in the morning sunshine. 'What else?'

'You're meeting Sam Tenbury to discuss the possibility of Softshare sponsoring a tennis tournament. You're having lunch together—'

'Where?'

Megan smiled confidently. She had asked one of the executive assistants for the name of the best local restaurant. And even the pernickety Dan McKnight surely couldn't find fault with her choice. 'I've booked that riverside restaurant—'

'Change it.'

'But—'

'Change it,' he repeated on a growl, meeting the bemused question in her eyes. 'I'm much too busy to have my time wasted by waiters who think that offering me an oversized pepper pot should be greeted with laughter and loud applause!'

Megan frowned. She had briefly gone out with a waiter while she was still at secretarial college and knew what long hours they put in for what amounted to little more than a meagre pittance. 'But they're only doing their job, Dan—'

'Yes, I know they are,' he said, with a quick, impatient smile. 'I just don't want it to interfere with mine! And it's the kind of restaurant where men take their mistresses—'

Megan looked up quickly. It was a very old-fashioned word for him to have used, she thought. And not a particularly flattering one. 'How do you work that one out—is there a sign on the door or something?'

'You've obviously never been there.'

'Well, I certainly wouldn't admit to it now—even if I had! What's wrong with it?'

'I just don't think it deserves its reputation as being the best place to eat locally. It's badly lit with corny music—the food is mediocre and it's overpriced. I don't want to browse through a menu of encyclopaedic length or have my wineglass filled every other second so that by the end of the meal I'm on my knees. I'm not planning a long, slow seduction—'

'Gosh! Sam Tenbury *will* be relieved!' she joked.

Dan sent her a glimmer of disapproval as he bit his words out. 'I just want to eat and then talk business.'

'Right.' Megan stared at him—all health and vitality in that grey suit which made his eyes look like glittering slate in comparison. 'Well, I really don't know any other restaurants in the area. Any suggestions?''

Dan plugged in his laptop. 'Why don't we eat here?'

Megan conjured up a vision of herself flitting in and out, carrying plates of sandwiches. Did he expect her to make them as well? 'What—in the office?'

He gave her the type of look he reserved for people who were being especially dense. 'No, Megan, not here in the office,' he answered sarcastically. 'I don't want crumbs in my keyboard! I meant the staff canteen.'

'Oh,' she said.

He heard the doubt in her voice. 'The food is good—and there's no chance of alcohol clouding our judgement, since the strongest liquid on sale is root beer!'

Poor old Sam Tenbury, thought Megan. If he thought he was about to have an extravagant time with one of the dynamic directors of Softshare he was about to be very disappointed! 'Right,' she said briskly. 'I'll cancel the table. Let's hope Sam wasn't expecting you to push the boat out!'

Dan looked at her with a faint air of disapproval. 'Why should he? You must know the company philosophy by now, Megan— how long have you been here? A month, is it?'

'Nearly three months actually,' she corrected pithily, wondering if he had deliberately cultivated the knack of making a woman feel completely invisible.

'And...' He sat down behind his desk and stretched his long legs out in front of him. 'What have you learned so far?'

Megan felt like a child asked to recite their times-tables in front of the teacher! 'That frugality is the name of the game,' she told him earnestly. 'That Softshare directors fly economy class. That you don't make your offices into palaces.'

'And why not?' he asked softly.

'Because you plough all the profits back into keeping ahead of your competitors,' she answered obediently.

'Mmm. Very good, Megan,' he said, looking closely at the screen in front of him.

'Do I go to the top of the class?' she wondered aloud.

But Dan wasn't listening; he was staring at the figures on his screen with the kind of rapt fascination which most men reserved for beautiful women.

The office was large and spacious and had been designed with the full cooperation of a design consultant. Two desks sat facing one another, which was not really Megan's idea of fun. Those cool grey eyes didn't exactly make you feel relaxed. And you certainly couldn't varnish your nails or telephone a girlfriend—even in your lunch hour—not when your boss was sitting only feet away!

The only respite she got was when Dan had to go away on business, which wasn't as often as she would have liked. Because, like most assistants, she found the office ran much better when her boss wasn't around!

In one corner of the room was a seating area which had made a couple of concessions towards comfort. It contained a sofa and two soft chairs, with a low table in between. Fresh flowers were sent each week by a florist and were subtle and scented. Clutter in the room had been kept to a minimum and Megan was trying to enter into the spirit of this new working environment. She had already 'streamlined' her desk, and eagerly studied the section of the Softshare manual which included guidelines on how to make your life less stressful. Though so far, at least, she wasn't sure if it was working.

They worked non-stop until Megan's stomach began to rumble. When Dan was working, he seemed to forget about such mundane matters as food and drink.

'Would you like some peppermint tea?' she asked hopefully. 'Or maybe you'd prefer camomile?'

Dan winced. 'No, I wouldn't! I'll have that coffee now—strong and black, the same as always.'

'But too much caffeine can make you irritable, Dan—'

'Yes, and *you* seem to be doing a pretty good job of that, too! Why on earth would I need coffee, Megan?' he snapped sarcastically as he checked his e-mail.

Megan went out to fetch him coffee served just the way he liked it—which was ebony-black without any sugar—and was presumably what kept him so alert. And so lean. She set it down on his desk in front of him, then ate a large green apple while Dan spoke at great length to someone in Tokyo, frowning at her every time she crunched.

After that he took a conference call. At noon Reception buzzed to say that Sam Tenbury was waiting downstairs, and Dan stretched his arms high above his head and gave a lazy yawn.

Megan found herself wondering who he had taken to the theatre with him and how late a night it had been afterwards. And also wondered if the lucky woman was the same woman who had penned the letter which still lay unopened in his in-tray. Megan gazed down at it, but Dan was already by the door and didn't appear to have noticed her pointed stare.

Anyway, it was none of her business.

'Okay, Megan. You know where I'll be. See you in about an hour,' he promised, and closed the office door quietly behind him.

The room felt a bit empty after he'd gone and Megan threw herself into organising an off-site meeting for the following month, where Softshare employees would congregate for one of the team-building programmes which the company promoted so fiercely.

She was just thinking about eating her own sandwich—which she always made up for herself at home before she drove her scooter into work—when the telephone rang and she picked it up.

'Hello, Dan McKnight's office, Megan speaking. How may I help?'

There was a breathy pause. And then a young woman's voice—asking a studiedly casual question which came out sounding as if it had been rehearsed over and over. 'Is he there, please? D-Dan, I mean.'

'I'm afraid not,' said Megan. 'He's out at a meeting.'

'Oh. Oh, I see.' The voice sounded *so* young and so crestfallen that all Megan's protective instincts came hustling to the surface.

'May I take a message?'

'Not really.'

'Or say who was calling?'

'No, no! That's okay. It doesn't matter. Honestly.'

But the girl sounded so dejected that Megan felt impelled to ask, 'Are you sure? I can get a message to him if you like. He'll be back very soon.'

A noise followed which sounded suspiciously like a gulp. 'Well, I don't know if it'll do any good...' The voice tailed off uncertainly.

Megan was not the oldest of five children for nothing—and she could tell when someone wanted to get something off their chest. 'Oh, go on,' she coaxed gently. 'You can tell me.'

'Well...um, do you know if he's been getting his mail?' asked the voice tentatively.

Certainty hit Megan like a slap to the face. This was the writer of the elaborate envelopes—she would bet her entire month's salary on that! But how could she admit to the woman that her letters had been arriving without also having to admit that Dan McKnight had been refusing to read them?

'Dan always has a great mountain of mail—electronic and conventional mail,' said Megan smoothly. No lies there. 'But he's been snowed under with work lately.' Which was also the truth. 'So he probably hasn't got around to reading them.' Now…did the fabrication sound as loud to the mystery caller's ears as it did to her own?

'Yes,' said the voice dejectedly. 'I guess that's why I haven't heard.'

'So why don't I have him call you when he gets back?'

There was a rather hollow laugh. 'No, that's okay. I'll be seeing him at the weekend. I'll talk to him then. Th-thanks for all your help.'

The connection was broken and Megan was left staring blankly down at the phone, but her protective instincts had been roused. She found herself logging appointments into Dan's diary with only half a mind on the task in hand, so that by the time he returned from his lunch she had worked out exactly what she was going to say to him.

Dan walked into the office to find his assistant looking puffed-up and slightly self-important, and began to wonder whether his satisfaction in her performance had been a little premature.

She'd been nothing but a pain this morning! The way she kept drawing his attention to those confounded letters—letters which were currently burning an uncomfortable hole in his conscience.

Yet, at her interview, Megan Phillips had not only displayed all the characteristics which Softshare specifically looked for in an employee, she'd had the added advantage of not being the type to stand out in a crowd, which was definitely a plus as far as Dan was concerned.

He'd had beautiful assistants before—women who seemed to think that a lovely face and stunning body would catapult them from their assistant's desk into the high-ranking security of the boss's bed!

Not that Megan Phillips was ugly, he conceded wryly. In fact, she came nowhere near being ugly—she was just refreshingly and unthreateningly ordinary. She didn't wear make-up and she didn't wear short skirts, either. In fact, she never wore skirts at all—always trousers. Presumably to cover up her fat ankles. And that was just fine by him.

Because Dan McKnight had one prime rule in business.

That he never slept with anyone he worked with.

Megan was itching to tell him about the phone call, but equally determined to be professional, so she toiled away all afternoon and waited until it was almost going-home time before she brought the subject up. 'Dan?'

'What?'

'Your girlfriend rang while you were out.'

He lifted his dark head and the grey eyes took on a wary expression. 'Really?'

'Really.' There was something about the tone of his voice which made her feel faintly uneasy. Megan blinked at him, waiting for some clarification—until she realised that she wasn't going to get any.

'Which girlfriend would that be?' he queried unhelpfully.

'You mean you've got more than *one*?' She couldn't keep the indignation out of her voice. Or the accusation.

There was a frosty shimmer of silence while Dan tussled with the idea of sending her packing right there and then, until common sense reasserted itself. And there were no absolutely no grounds for sacking your assistant just because she thought you had an overgrown libido! Maybe he should be flattered by it!

'I have lots of friends of both sexes,' came the silky correction. 'Don't you?'

'Er, yes,' stumbled Megan, feeling slightly foolish. 'Of course I do.'

He continued to look at her questioningly. 'So who was it?'

Horror dawned on her as she realised that she hadn't even asked the woman's name! 'Er, I don't know.'

'You don't know?' he repeated ominously.

'No.'

'You didn't think to take a name?'

'Well, I—'

'Aren't you aware that taking incomplete messages is one of the most irritating traits known to mankind?' he demanded heatedly. 'It's bad enough in a flatmate—but in an assistant it becomes more than merely irritating, it veers into the realms of sheer incompetence!'

Megan felt torn between protecting her job and protecting the woman on the telephone— even though the job was the best-paid she had ever had, and she didn't know the woman from a bar of soap.

But…sisterhood, and all that.

Which was presumably why she found herself staring fearlessly into those grey eyes and saying, 'She told me she'd written to you, but said that you hadn't bothered to reply.'

He saw that her gaze was now burning into the top drawer of his desk where he'd stashed the stack of pastel-coloured envelopes in the hope that they might somehow go away if he ignored them for long enough.

'Oh, did she?' he asked, in a voice so soft that Megan failed to notice the dangerous undertone to it. 'And what else did she say?'

'That she would see you this weekend, and talk to you then.'

Dan let out a long, resigned sigh. 'I see.'

Megan made one last attempt in the name of female solidarity. 'She sounded very… upset, Dan.'

He correctly latched onto the disapproval in her voice. 'And?' he questioned silkily.

Megan blinked. He seemed to be asking her opinion, so why not give it? Wasn't that what she was being paid to do? 'I think you owe it to her to at least do her the courtesy of replying.'

Dan almost laughed aloud at what was, in fact, a beautifully worded insult. From his *assistant*, no less!

'Oh, do you?' he questioned, keeping his irritation at bay with difficulty. 'And didn't it occur to you that there might be a reason why I've let them all go unanswered?'

'Some men play hard to get,' suggested Megan boldly. 'Treat them mean to keep them keen! Maybe you're one of those men?'

'I can see that I've already reached dizzy heights in your estimation of me,' he said sarcastically.

'It was only an option,' Megan shrugged. 'I don't really know you very well.'

'No, you don't!' he grated. 'Because if you did you would know that my ego isn't in any way fragile! And that I certainly don't need to encourage the attention of lovelorn teenagers in order to get my kicks!'

'Teenagers?' asked Megan in a voice so shocked that Dan glared at her some more. 'Lovelorn?'

'Well, there's no need to sound *quite* so outraged!' he defended as he clipped the words out. 'I'm thirty-three years old—not quite at the stage of queuing up for my pension book. Anyway, she's nearly twenty.'

Megan tried to sound worldly-wise. 'And you've been having an affair with her, have you?'

Maybe it was the fact that he wasn't used to people he barely knew making negative character assessments about him that made him feel so uncharacteristically angry. But whatever it was—in that moment, Dan felt like striding across the office and *shaking* her!

'Bloody hell!' he swore. 'You're making me sound like Bluebeard! No, I have *not* been having an affair with her—cradle-snatching has never turned me on!'

'Well, what is it, then?' asked Megan in confusion. 'What's her name, and what's it all about?'

Dan sighed. He kept his private life just that. Private. But if Katrina had started phoning and writing to him here, then inevitably his professional life would be involved. And compromised, too, if he wasn't careful.

'Her name is Katrina,' he said. 'And she thinks she's in love with me.'

'Why?'

In spite of everything, Dan laughed. He threw his dark head back and let rip with a throaty chuckle as her question brought him crashing down to earth. Because if his ego had been threatening to get out of hand that guileless one-word query had checked it! But then he saw the reproach which had clouded those huge hazel eyes of hers, and felt his temper flare. Again.

'Why do you think?' he demanded. 'Because I had my wicked way with her when she was barely out of nappies?'

'Dan!'

'Well, that's what the prissy look of concern on your face is implying, isn't it, Megan?'

'No!'

'And you've obviously taken her side—'

'I haven't taken anyone's side! I felt sorry for her, that was all.'

'Even though,' he continued furiously, his grey eyes growing thunder-dark, 'even though you don't know her and you barely know me? In fact, you don't have a clue about the true situation!'

'Maybe I don't,' she agreed. 'But that's easily remedied. Why don't you tell me?'

Dan's mouth flattened into a thin, hard line, and he stared at her with misgiving. He had been brought up to view the airing of emotions as a weakness—while to take a virtual stranger into his confidence would be interpreted as positively indulgent.

But he couldn't just carry on ignoring a situation which was threatening to spiral out of control, could he? And Megan had no axe to grind. She didn't know Katrina. She stood to gain nothing by giving him her opinion. Surely it would not be disloyal to confide in his assistant?

'Maybe I *should* tell you,' he said slowly.

But, even so, Megan was amazed when Dan sat back in his chair and studied her intently from between narrowed eyes, the way he sometimes studied a spreadsheet.

'Okay.' He nodded, and gave a smile which managed to be angry and thoughtful all at the same time. 'I will. I'll tell you the whole story about Katrina and then we'll see where your sympathies lie, won't we, Megan?'

CHAPTER TWO

'PICTURE the scene,' said Dan, and picked up the smooth round paperweight which lay on his desk. At its centre sat a small pink shell and usually he found it restful to look at. Not today, though. 'Of a little girl growing up without any men around.'

Megan watched him run his long fingers over the cool, curved glass. What he was describing was the exact reverse of her own upbringing. There had been men galore around—or boys, to be exact—when she had slipped into the role of caring for her four younger brothers.

But she knew that having your mother die in childhood wasn't typical. Thank God. She pushed away the poignant memories and looked into his cool grey eyes. 'This is Katrina we're talking about, I presume?'

'That's right.' He nodded. 'She and her mother used to live close to us. My mother is her godmother, and I've known Katrina for most of her life.'

'Right,' nodded Megan cautiously.

'She is the daughter of an actress who happens to be very, very beautiful—'

Megan found herself wondering whether Katrina was as beautiful as her mother. But she didn't ask.

'And very self-obsessed,' he continued, only now the edges of his voice were roughened with disapproval. 'And, like many beautiful women, she regarded the arrival of a daughter as something of a catastrophe—'

'Oh.' Megan's eyes widened. 'Why?'

He seemed faintly taken aback by the genuine surprise in her question. Didn't she realise how competitive women could be? He looked at her. No. Maybe she didn't.

'Because daughters have a habit of growing up!' he answered. 'They provide the physical evidence of how quickly the years are passing, don't they? And there's nothing an actress hates more than growing old. You can't carry on pretending to be in your mid-thirties if you have daughter who is in her twenties!'

'No, I suppose you can't,' said Megan slowly. 'I never thought of it like that.' She looked at him, fascinated by what he was telling her. Dan McKnight, of all people, pouring his heart out—why, she hadn't thought he had one! 'So where do you fit into the picture?'

Dan had recently been asking himself the same question, searching back in his memory for something he might have said or done which could have been misinterpreted by a naive young girl.

He frowned. 'Ever since Katrina was a little girl, she latched herself onto me and followed me around the place, whenever I was around. Which wasn't often enough for her to see for herself that idols often have feet of clay,' he added, with brutal honesty.

'You mean you were her idol?'

He thought it might sound unacceptably arrogant if he corrected her sentence from past to present tense. 'I guess I was.' He also thought that Megan could have taken that note of astonishment out of her voice. 'She used to trot round beside me, gazing up at me as though I could do no wrong.' And he would be lying to himself if he denied that he had liked the young girl. And enjoyed her unconditional adoration. It had worked both ways—because Katrina had been like the little sister he'd never had.

And that was part of the problem. You could tell a sister to go away and she would probably listen to you.

'So what did you do about it?' she asked.

Dan sighed, accepting now that he might have adopted entirely the wrong strategy. He had thought that, by ignoring the young girl's obsession with him, she would grow out of it, the way she'd grown out of having puppy fat. 'Nothing,' he admitted. 'I just acted exactly the same as I always had towards her.'

'And how was that?'

'Big-brotherly, I suppose.'

'So there was no attraction between you at all?'

Dan shook his dark head. 'Not on my part, certainly! The age difference between us is too great for us to have anything in common—apart from geographical proximity, of course.'

Megan nodded, looking closely at the cool, clever face. 'And what is the age difference, exactly?'

'Thirteen years.'

She expelled a long breath. 'It *is* a big gap, but it's not unheard of,' offered Megan, thinking of Hollywood stars and minor royals.

'Neither is slave labour, but that doesn't make it all right!' Dan threw her an impatient look. 'Think about it! When she was a chubby five-year-old, I was just setting off for university. So do you really think that we *bonded*? Maybe you imagine that every time I came home we sat down and discussed which brand of chocolate bar we liked best!'

Megan opened her mouth to say that she didn't know why he seemed to be taking it out on *her*. But she shut it again. Dan McKnight was usually so elusive about his personal life. Getting information was often like prising a clam out of its shell. So if he was now choosing to open up to her, then she should be flattered as well as intrigued. 'Of course I don't think that,' she said calmly.

Her composure seemed to take the heat out of some of his anger, and he put the paperweight down on top of a sheaf of papers. 'Anyway,' he shrugged. 'By the time she'd reached fifteen, I was twenty-eight—'

'And I suppose the age difference became far less significant as you both got older,' suggested Megan reflectively.

Dan gave her another thoughtful look. 'That's certainly what Katrina thought.'

'So did…?' Megan chose her words carefully. 'Did she just suddenly *decide* that she was in love with you—or did something happen?'

His eyelashes brushed together, obscuring and shadowing his eyes. 'Like what?'

'Well—'

'You think I made a pass at her?'

'No, of course I don't.' She tried to be diplomatic. 'Well, not intentionally, maybe…'

Dan felt the ticking of a slow rage as he met the mild suggestion in her eyes. Until he realised that maybe he wasn't as blameless as he'd imagined. It couldn't have all come out of nothing, could it? So had he—maybe subliminally—been sending out the wrong sort of message to Katrina for years? He thought back and shook his head. 'No,' he said firmly. 'I never did anything which could have been taken the wrong way.'

'So can you remember exactly when it started to get more serious?'

He tried to pinpoint the moment when a schoolgirl crush had begun to escalate out of control. 'I gave her a necklace on her eighteenth birthday,' he realised. 'It started soon afterwards.'

'And how long ago was that?'

'Almost two years.'

So Katrina was persistent. Two years of unrequited love was certainly dedication. 'What kind of necklace?' she asked.

'Seed-pearls,' he answered slowly, remembering that he'd bought them on his mother's recommendation, and that they had cost rather more than he had intended to pay. He remembered the way Katrina had looked at him when he had handed the slim package over. The stunned expression followed by the shining gratitude in her eyes. The way she had flung her arms so tightly around his neck, until he had eventually had to disentangle them. 'They were rather nice pearls, actually.'

'Well, then—*that's* why!' said Megan. 'You sent out the wrong message.'

He raised his eyebrows. 'How?'

'Women look at jewellery in a rather different way to men,' she explained. 'I mean—

you probably thought that you were just helping commemorate a big birthday, with a
pretty keepsake, from a friend—'

'Precisely!'

'Whereas women view certain pieces of
jewellery as actually *meaning* something.'
She looked at him. Even she knew *that*—
why, she still felt positively misty-eyed when
she put her own string of pearls on—though
that might be because they had belonged to
her mother. 'What made you buy them in the
first place?'

Dan shifted in his seat, beginning to feel
as though something had been going on that
he hadn't really been aware of. As though, in
some very discreet way, he'd been cleverly
manipulated. Why had he never seen the obvious link before? 'My mother suggested it.'

'Oh, I see.' She looked at him with a question in her eyes. 'Your mother obviously
likes her.'

'She *approves* of her, yes,' answered Dan
thoughtfully as he reflected on Megan's
words. 'So Katrina thinks she's in love with
me because I bought her a piece of fairly expensive jewellery for her eighteenth birthday?'

Megan faced him. 'You're the only one who can answer that.'

'So what do I do?'

'You make her stop loving you.'

'How?' he demanded.

Megan was tempted to suggest that he spend longer in the girl's company—that would be bound to make the dream evaporate in an instant!

'What have you done so far?' she questioned. 'To put her off?'

'Last time I saw her, I gently explained that the age difference between us is too great.'

Megan shook her head. 'Oh, dear! *Big* mistake!'

He looked at her sharply. 'Oh?'

'Saying that makes it sound as though it's only convention standing in your way! True love thwarted by an inflexible world! The Romeo and Juliet syndrome,' she added helpfully. 'What else have you done?'

'I don't take her phone calls any more—and I haven't returned any of the more recent e-mails. Or answered any of the letters.' He stared at the paperweight and when he looked up the grey eyes were troubled. 'Because I

can't think what to say—and because the letters are becoming slightly more—' he
seemed to have difficulty choosing the right
word '—*graphic*,' he finished reluctantly.

'Ignoring her will only make her more des-
perate,' Megan mused aloud, deciding that
there was absolutely no need for her to know
just *how* graphic. 'And she'll be worried that
she'll lose your friendship altogether. No, ignoring her won't help.'

'Well, then, just what *do* you suggest I
do?' he demanded.

Megan stared at him, her lips twitching
with the temptation to tell him that it wasn't
really her place to suggest anything at all.

But then she thought of Katrina's crestfallen voice and tried putting herself in the
girl's shoes and felt an enormous wave of
sympathy for her. Because hadn't she read
somewhere that obsessional love could gnaw
away at you and dominate your whole life?

She frowned with concentration. 'There is
one way of getting her off your back.' She
saw him wince at the way she had phrased
it. 'But you might think it's rather cruel.'

His eyes grew suspicious. 'What did you
have in mind?'

Megan smiled. Her brothers were the same. Couldn't see a simple solution even if it was staring them in the face!

'You just convince her that you're in love with someone else. Simple.'

'Oh, really?' he queried softly. 'And how do you propose I do that?'

'She said something about seeing you this weekend—'

'No. Let's rephrase that. You make it sound like a date and it's not. My brother is getting married in a few weeks' time—and he and his fiancée are visiting my mother's house this weekend. I planned to go along as well. And Katrina will be there, too.'

'So you take somebody else with you.' There was a marked lack of understanding in the cool grey eyes. 'A girlfriend,' she elaborated. 'Show Katrina you're all over somebody else! There's no surer way for someone to get the message that you aren't interested!'

'But I'm not in love with anybody else.'

Megan sighed. Men could be so infuriatingly dense at times—even ones as startlingly bright as Dan McKnight! 'You don't have to be. You just have to *pretend* to be. Just find someone who's willing to go along with it.'

Dan screwed his face up. 'Like who, for example?'

'Well, *I* don't know! There must be hundreds of women who would be delighted to slip into the role of being Dan McKnight's partner for the weekend!'

'Yes. With most of them looking to make the post permanent. I can't take the risk,' he said grimly.

His arrogance almost took her breath away. 'I'm sure there must be a woman *somewhere* who could manage to resist your charm for forty-eight hours, Dan!'

He acknowledged her sarcasm with a slight quirk of his lips, and then his grey eyes began to gleam with the first inkling of a plan. Someone outside his circle. Someone who would be willing to play along with it for a couple of days and then forget it. Someone who didn't tempt him. Someone who...

'How about you?' he asked suddenly.

'*Me?*' Megan stared at him. 'Why me?'

He considered this. There was no point in beating about the bush. 'Well, the main reason is because you don't find me in any way attractive.' His eyes bored into her. 'Do you, Megan?'

Megan stared back at him. She knew that nine women out of ten would have fancied him. Maybe if she hadn't worked for him she might have felt differently. As it was, she found it easier to imagine being kissed by a block of concrete than by Dan McKnight. She shook her head. 'No, I don't.'

Dan smiled. 'Thank you for not bothering to spare my feelings,' he murmured. 'And, fortunately, the feeling is entirely mutual. You're probably the last woman in the world I would choose to have a relationship with.'

Megan glared. Surely there were nicer ways he could have put it? 'Thanks very much!'

He flicked her a look from between the dark curtain of his lashes. 'So. Are you busy this weekend?'

Megan hesitated. There was a sort of unspoken rule that if you were a single woman and a man asked if you were busy you always said that, yes, you were. Very. From this, they would come to the conclusion that you had a wonderful, exciting life of your own and you weren't just sitting around waiting for Mr Wonderful to come galloping into it on his white charger.

But Megan had always had a problem with telling lies. Even if they *were* only tiny ones.

'Er, no. I'm not. I'm free, actually.'

'So would you do it, Megan?'

'Pretend to be your love-struck girlfriend, you mean?'

'That's right.'

Megan looked at him. At the cool grey eyes and the thick, dark hair. At the body which was surprisingly lean and muscular for a man who didn't have a job which was fundamentally physical. 'No,' she said flatly.

Dan's eyes widened. He wasn't the kind of man who often had to ask a woman for a favour—those were usually offered freely enough. Neither was he used to being turned down quite so firmly or so emphatically as Megan Phillips had just done, and he suddenly found the novelty of being refused almost stimulating.

And certainly surprising.

'Why not?' he asked.

'Because I'm your assistant—I can't go along pretending to be your lover.'

'I wasn't actually expecting you to consummate our fictitious relationship.' He bit back a smile. 'That would be taking method acting a little too far!'

If Megan hadn't grown up on a farm and been so matter-of-fact about the act of procreation, then she might well have been embarrassed by a remark she suspected had been made with just that aim in mind. As it was, she was able to return his mocking stare with an unruffled look of her own. 'I hardly know anything about you.'

'You seem to have extracted a lot more information than most people,' he told her truthfully.

'Not enough if we're supposed to be in love.'

'Ask me anything you want,' he coaxed softly.

'What would I have to do?'

'Very little. Eat a few meals with me. Maybe play a little tennis. Laugh at my jokes. Withstand the third degree from my mother. Gaze adoringly into my eyes—'

'I don't know about the gazing adoringly into your eyes bit,' she told him honestly. 'I'm not that good an actress!'

He pursed his lips together, like someone who'd been amused by an unexpected source of entertainment. 'Well, if the pleasure of my company doesn't tempt you enough, here's an added inducement.' He paused for effect before saying softly, 'What if I told you that a very famous actor was also going to be there this weekend?'

Slightly relieved that he hadn't done anything so vulgar as offer her money, Megan willed herself not to look *too* interested. He probably meant somebody who'd been in a series of coffee advertisements. 'Oh? And who's that?'

Dan enjoyed the moment. 'Jake Haddon.'

Megan's face froze in disbelieving surprise. It was a full ten seconds before she could speak. '*The* Jake Haddon?'

'Is there more than one?'

Megan swallowed, more confused than excited. Because not only had Jake Haddon just starred in the year's biggest-grossing film— but the upper-class Englishman with a fine line in irony had been voted the sexiest star of the decade!

'Jake *Haddon*,' she questioned slowly, speaking each word with extreme care, just in case she had misheard him, 'is actually going to be at your mother's house?'

'That's right.'

Megan frowned. In her world, famous actors didn't just happen to stay with your parents. 'Is he a friend of yours?' she asked suspiciously.

'Yes, he is.' He saw the disbelieving look in her eyes and felt obliged to elaborate. 'He grew up locally. We went to the same village school for a while, before he moved away. But we always kept in touch.'

What sort of world did he inhabit, she wondered, if he was mixing with people of *that* calibre and had never let on about it? Why, if Jake Haddon were *her* friend, she'd have his posters plastered all over the office walls!

As Dan spoke, he watched the excitement working Megan's face—an excitement she was unsuccessfully trying to suppress. And he wondered why he should feel an odd twinge of disappointment that she should be so transparent.

Had he imagined that she would differ from other women, by not being attracted to a man because of who he was, rather than what he was? When would he ever learn? His mouth turned down at the corners. 'So. Changed your mind about coming?'

Megan knew that she shouldn't be swayed by a famous name. And instinctively—for whatever reason—she suspected that part of Dan *wanted* her to say no.

Say no? She would have to be locked up first! She very nearly leapt up and down with excitement. Just wait until she told her brothers about *this*! 'I certainly have!'

'So you'll come?'

'Yes, please!'

'Oh, the hypnotic lure of celebrity,' he murmured drily.

'It'll be something to tell my grandchildren!' she defended.

'Just make sure they're not Jake's grandchildren, too,' he warned. He saw the confused look on her face grow into one of indignation as she worked out what he meant by *that* remark. 'He has, er, something of a reputation with women,' he added quickly. 'As I am sure you can imagine.'

She wasn't surprised. Looking the way Jake Haddon did, he probably had to surround himself with an army of minders! Still, actors who were constantly being offered big bucks by Hollywood did not tend to run after unsophisticated assistants who'd grown up on a pig-farm!

Megan leaned back in her chair and curved her mouth into a wide smile. 'So. A heart-throb actor and a man who is being emotion-ally stalked by a woman he can't bear to hurt.' She let out a sigh of anticipation. 'This looks like being one hell of a weekend!'

CHAPTER THREE

MEGAN felt quite light-headed as she pulled on her motorcycle helmet after work. The summer evening was still and heavy, and there was a sense of unreality nagging away at her, as if she couldn't quite believe that she'd just agreed to go away with Dan McKnight and pretend to be his loving partner!

She climbed onto the scooter which her father and brothers had clubbed together to buy for her twenty-first birthday, as a thank-you for all she'd done for them. Its top speed wasn't much faster than some of the runners she passed as they jogged along the pavements—but it was an easy way to get home at the end of a long day.

Home was half a small house which she shared with another girl, close to the Softshare building and just half an hour's train journey away from Central London.

When Megan had left her father's farm, she'd planned to go into the capital itself—

but the exorbitant price of renting and the mad, busy pace of life had put her off. It had seemed too big and too noisy after the peace of the countryside she had grown up in.

At first, she'd rented a microscopically small bedsit—but then she'd started going out with David and was rarely at home, so size hadn't seemed to matter. And when they'd split up, she'd decided that she needed company. As a parting gesture, David had offered to buy her a cat, but Megan had declined the offer and found herself a house-mate instead!

The house was tucked away in a road which ran parallel to the main street. There were trees along one side, and when the shops were closed it was quiet—but parking was nearly always a nightmare, and Megan thanked her lucky stars that her little scooter was so easy to park!

And this place had been a terrific compromise, she reasoned, letting herself in the front door. Green enough to almost imagine that you were in the country, yet close enough to London to feel that your finger was still on the pulse.

'Hel-*lo*!' she called as she rifled through the post lying on the hall table, and found only a letter of the 'we are sure this is merely an oversight' variety, asking her to settle up the interest on her in-store account. Maybe her accountant brother was right. Maybe she just shouldn't *have* an in-store account!

'I'm out here!' shouted a voice. 'In the kitchen!'

The kitchen was scruffy, but at least it had French doors looking out onto the tiny garden, which in the summer was a glorious suntrap. Megan had laboriously grown packets of seeds on the kitchen window-sill, and now they were planted proudly in their pots outside—blazing with colour and heavy with scent. A heavy-headed sunflower strained its giant yellow petals towards the sky and cute little black-eyed Susans winked at her provocatively.

Helen was standing by the fridge, hulling strawberries which she was piling into a scarlet pyramid on a glass dish. She was a pretty, bubbly girl who worked as a flight attendant for one of the major airlines, so she had lots of stopovers in places like Paris and Madrid and Rome, which she insisted *weren't* glamorous—but which sounded it to Megan! She was currently unattached, even though she always seemed to have hundreds of admirers—but she told Megan she was holding out for the 'real thing'.

Helen looked up as Megan walked in and stopped chopping once she saw the expression on her housemate's face. 'What's up?' she demanded. 'Has something happened?'

'Well, kind of.' Megan paused for effect as she anticipated the impact that her next words would have. 'What would you say if I told you that I was going to spend the weekend in the company of the actor Jake Haddon?'

The knife only narrowly missed Helen's thumb. She put it down on the work surface carefully. 'I'd say that you had either been hit on the head or had started dating someone who just happened to share their name with the hunky actor we all know and love!'

Megan picked up half a strawberry and popped it into her mouth. 'Well, you'd be wrong. Because Jake Haddon—*the* Jake Haddon—is actually going to be there.'

Helen stared at her in genuine confusion. 'Where?'

'It's a bit of an odd story.'

'You don't say?' Helen picked the kettle up. 'Tell me all about it while I make some tea.'

Fifteen minutes later, the cooling kettle was left forgotten on the work surface and Helen stared at Megan, her eyes as wide as dinner-plates.

'You're sure this isn't some ploy by your new boss to have his wicked way with you?'

Megan nearly choked on the second-to-last strawberry. 'Have you *seen* him?'

'No. Why? Is he vile?'

Megan shook her head, and almost laughed. 'No, he's not vile. He's just...'

Helen stood waiting expectantly. 'Just what?'

Megan shrugged. 'Nothing. It just wouldn't happen,' she said firmly. 'I'm not interested in him, and he's certainly not interested in *me*. He even told me so!'

'Really?' Helen nodded. 'That's why he's taking you away and having you pretend to be in love with him, is it?'

'It isn't like that!'

'Hmm. Maybe. I know men—'

'And so do I!' Megan protested. 'I grew up in a house full of them, remember?'

'Yes, and they were your devoted and very protective brothers and father. Not men with an eye for the main chance.' Helen gave her a speculative look. 'What on earth are you going to wear? And isn't he going to get a shock when he sees you out of your habitual trousers?'

'Probably—especially when he notices my skinny knees!'

'How many times do I have to keep telling you there's nothing wrong with skinny knees? Most women yearn for them! Models have them! And you still haven't answered the question about what to wear. Lets face it, Megan, your wardrobe isn't exactly full to overflowing with any kind of clothes—let alone suitable clothes for what sounds like a very fancy weekend in the country.'

'No, I know it isn't.' Megan gave her a slightly embarrassed smile. 'Um, shall I make us that cup of tea now?'

Helen burst out laughing. 'You mean, you want to borrow some clothes?'

'Well, we *are* about the same size. Would you mind?'

'Mind? I've been dying to see what you'd look like in something really funky for ages now. Come on—what are you waiting for?'

Minutes later, Megan stood in front of a full-length mirror looking over her shoulder at a bottom which seemed far from perfect when it was covered in tight buttercup-yellow satin.

'Helen, I can't wear these!' she said flatly.

'Of course you can! They're very young and very *now*—and satin is the new denim, didn't you know?' Helen stepped back admiringly. 'I must say, they make a *wild* pair of jeans!'

'Wild,' echoed Megan weakly. 'I just don't know if it's going to be that sort of weekend.'

'Didn't you ask him?'

'Of course I asked him!'

'And what did he say about it—this Dan McKnight?'

'Just that his mother would be there—'

'His *mother*?'

'That's right. And his brother—'

'Oh, wow! Sounds like a fun time,' observed Helen wryly. Megan ignored that. 'He said we'd get down there in time for dinner on the Friday and travel back after lunch on

Sunday. He said that Friday-night dinner was smartish but that they tended to dress up for dinner on Saturday. And that everything else was pretty relaxed.'

'And nothing else?'

'Not really. Just the bit about the girl who thinks she's in love with him. And about Jake Haddon being there, too.'

'Well, then! Actors! You can't turn up wearing a pair of those drab old trousers you usually wear, can you? He'll expect you to look bright. Colourful. Different.'

'Do you really think so?'

'Listen,' smiled Helen, 'I *know* so. Now take this sequinned boob-tube and go and try it on with these pedal-pushers!'

Megan looked down at the garments Helen had thrust into her hands, and frowned. 'Listen, I know I'm not the world's greatest fashion queen—'

'Agreed!'

'But even *I* know that pink doesn't really go with green—'

'Doesn't *go* with it? Darling, they were *made* for each other! Clashing colours are big news this season.'

'Honestly?'

'Trust me on this one, Megan.'

In the end, Megan gave up trying to convince Helen that, while she was dying to meet the actor, she certainly wasn't entertaining any false expectations about him falling for her.

'He wouldn't look twice at someone like me!' she declared stoutly.

'No,' agreed Helen thoughtfully. 'He most probably wouldn't. Not at the moment, anyway...' And she began to advance on her housemate carrying a mascara wand like a dangerous weapon.

'What are you doing?' asked Megan, in alarm.

'Seeing what you look like with a bit of slap on your face!'

Soon Megan's bed was covered with a selection of brightly coloured clothes and the face which stared back at her from the mirror was unrecognisable.

Her green-gold eyes looked three times their usual size and her skin looked as softly glowing as if she had just returned from a Mediterranean cruise. Her lips were all kind of tremulous and pouting with that carefully applied pink shiny stuff gleaming back at her.

And even her mousy-brown hair looked interesting after Helen had attacked it with a hairdryer.

But Megan wasn't sure that she liked this sleek, polished stranger who stared back at her from the mirror, and started wiping off the bronze blusher which she privately thought made her look as if she'd overdone the sunbed.

She was just throwing a used piece of cotton wool into the bin when the pile of clothes caught her eye, and she frowned. What if they'd judged it all wrong? Shouldn't she take her one, plain, all-purpose 'good' black dress? Just in case. If the worst came to the worst, she could dress it down for Friday, and tart it up for Saturday.

Feeling a little like a conspirator, she stuffed it into the bottom of her suitcase—where Helen couldn't see it.

Back in the office, Megan found herself looking at Dan in a whole new way. It was difficult not to. Here was a man who could inspire obsessional devotion from young women and who mixed with Oscar-nominated actors! She tried to be objective. Was he a hunk or not?

She supposed that he really *did* have an amazing bone-structure, when you looked closely. And pretty amazing eyes, too. But she soon forced herself to break the habit of staring and trying to analyse his appeal. What if he caught her doing it and thought that she was nurturing a soft spot for him? She had been expressly invited because she was the type of woman who *wouldn't* fall in love with him for real!

That week he had business in Spain and Holland, and came back the day before they were due to leave. Megan had spent most of the morning fixing up the quarterly review meeting and had looked up to find his grey eyes studying her intently, in a way she'd never noticed him doing before. It was an odd kind of sensation and for a moment she felt extremely flustered.

'Is something wrong?' she asked. He was probably having second thoughts—deciding that it had all been a mad, crazy idea, and that he didn't want to take her away with him after all.

She would never meet his mother and brother or get to know Jake Haddon.

And she was unprepared for the jolt of disappointment she experienced.

'Wrong?' He looked mildly surprised. 'Why should there be?'

'You were staring.'

'Was I?'

'You know you were.'

There was a pause.

'So I was,' he agreed softly. 'Is that such a crime?'

'Of course not,' said Megan stiffly, trying not to feel self-conscious in her pale grey cotton trousers and the darker grey T-shirt.

'Clearly it is,' he contradicted silkily, and there was a question in his eyes she couldn't ignore.

'I don't dress to be stared at,' she said defensively. 'Particularly not when I'm working.'

'No, I can see that,' he agreed, thinking that she wouldn't have looked out of place as a guard in a large institution, wearing that dreary outfit. Her top was so loose she might almost have been in the early stages of pregnancy! 'Still—it's refreshing to meet a woman who has such little vanity,' he smiled.

Megan frowned. Somehow she didn't like the sound of that.

He saw the lines which pleated her smooth, pale forehead and thought he'd better get in a bit of practice at making polite conversation. 'So. Are you looking forward to the weekend?'

'I'm not sure,' she admitted.

Actually, she'd been besieged with doubts. Lying awake at night staring at the ceiling and practising what on earth she would say to Jake Haddon when she met him. Which was only slightly less nerve-racking than imagining what she was going to say to Dan's mother!

'I'm just a bit nervous about having to keep making up stories. I hate lying, that's all. What have you told your family?'

'I spoke to my brother and told him that I'm bringing a girl home.'

'And that's all?'

'Believe me, that was enough.' His smile was cool as he remembered his brother's surprised silence down the telephone. 'The very fact that I'm bringing someone to a family party will be enough to convince them that it's serious enough to set alarm bells ringing.'

'Alarm bells?' she asked him curiously. 'Why should it do that? Don't they want you to settle down and get married?'

'I don't know—I've never asked them.'

Megan frowned. 'Must you be so *evasive* all the time?'

'Am I?' Dan frowned, too. 'Really?'

'Yes, really—you're about as forthcoming as a rock!'

'We've never discussed marriage,' he answered eventually, realising as he said it that he and his family had never discussed anything much at all. It wasn't their way. 'I suppose the unspoken fact is that when I do...'

'Yes?' quizzed Megan eagerly.

'It'll be someone from the same background, I guess.'

She didn't like to ask what that background was—but she was slowly getting a good idea!

'How rigid!' she observed.

'Not really,' he shrugged, and crumpled a ball of paper in his fist. 'Just stop and think about it. Marriage can be such a lottery. At least if you have similar backgrounds and interests, you stand a better chance of surviving.'

'You make it sound like a trip to the North Pole!' declared Megan indignantly. 'Marriage is supposed to be based on love!'

He smiled. 'I would hate to destroy your youthful idealism, Megan.'

'Whereas I would *love* to destroy your world-weary cynicism!'

He laughed, thinking that maybe this weekend wasn't going to be as bad as he had anticipated, until he drew himself up short.

This wasn't a date! he reminded himself sternly.

Megan took a call from their Rome office and put it through to him, and when the call was finished she plucked up courage to ask the question which had been depriving her of more sleep than any other. 'Er, Dan?'

He lifted his head. 'What?'

It wasn't the easiest thing to put into words, particularly when he was looking at her with that barely feigned impatience. 'It's a bit of a thorny subject—'

'I'm listening.'

'And it's probably only because I'm a farmer's daughter and don't feel shy to talk about one of the most basic—'

'Get to the point, will you, Megan?' he sighed.

She stared at him defiantly. 'It's about the sex thing.'

Dan blinked in astonishment and, as she spoke, the most extraordinary thing happened. He started to feel extremely... He shook his head in disbelief. Then shook it again—this time in astonishment. Surely the pale and colourless Ms Phillips hadn't managed to produce a sudden sweet flood of desire?

He shifted uncomfortably, pleased that he was safely hidden behind his desk so she couldn't see him. Imagine how embarrassing *that* would have been!

For both of them.

'Which particular aspect of the ''sex thing'' did you have in mind, exactly?' He swallowed.

'Well, it's just that if I'm supposed to be in love with you—'

'Yes?'

'And you with me...'

He looked at her as she let her sentence tail off, and he could feel his pulse begin to quicken again with another unexpected and completely unwanted challenge. 'Yes?' he said again, only this time he didn't bother to conceal his impatience.

'People will expect us—'

'To be having sex?' he put in brutally. 'No doubt they will, Megan—but that doesn't mean that they'll expect to witness it! Or do you think they'll be trooping through the house, expecting to see us locked together in the throes of passion? Much more interesting than looking at the paintings, wouldn't you say?'

Her throat constricted as her mind made pictures of his words. 'Is there really any need to be quite so…?'

Their eyes met. 'So?'

'Graphic?'

'Well, you were the one who started it! You're the farmer's daughter who claims to be unembarrassed by basic acts of nature, remember?' He smiled. 'Megan, stop worrying. We probably won't even be sleeping in the same part of the house.'

Megan blinked. 'Just how big *is* your house?'

'My mother is a stickler for convention,' he explained, as if she hadn't spoken. 'And, as far as she is concerned, unmarried couples just don't sleep together. Even my brother and his fiancée will have separate rooms. What they get up to in the dead of night is up to them!'

'And don't you mind?'

'Why should I mind? I don't visit *that* often—and I'm not so addicted to sex that I can't go without it for a night or two.'

Megan quickly found something very interesting to look at on the notepad in front of her.

Dan's gaze grew thoughtful. 'Don't worry. We'll play one of those cool, controlled couples who keep their passion firmly under wraps! We'll send each other occasional sizzling looks across the table so that the tension can build. But nothing more explicit. Do you think you can cope with that?'

'I suppose so.'

It occurred to Dan that there were more diplomatic ways she could have put it. Or maybe it was just the expression on her face—as if she were facing a session of root canal work at the dentist's—which was such a snub to his ego! 'Shouldn't you have laid down your terms and conditions *before* you agreed to do all this?' he demanded drily.

Megan met his stare. 'Maybe I should,' she agreed. 'In which case, maybe I'd better lay some down now.'

He leaned back in his chair. 'Go on.'

'I'm a naturally chatty person—'

'I'd noticed.'

'Whereas you tend to have something of a problem with communication.'

His gaze was sardonic. 'I work with computers and I'm a man—does that explain it?'

Megan smiled. 'You are also my boss, right?'

'So?'

'So, for the purposes of this weekend, we're going to have to suspend the normal rules of conduct.'

'You make this sound like a battle we're waging.'

Megan smiled. 'If I ask you a friendly question, I would prefer a friendly reply to a filthy look. Think you can manage to do that, Dan?'

'I can't see too much of a problem with that, Megan,' he replied gravely.

'And you mustn't start pulling rank—this weekend we're equals. We can say what we like to each other. Only—anything that happens this weekend will be instantly forgotten by Monday morning, when we revert back to normal. How does that sound?'

He frowned. 'And will my car turn back into a pumpkin?'

'I know why you're frowning,' she breezed on. 'It's because you're the kind of man who always lays down the rules, and you aren't used to someone else doing it for you—especially if she's a woman. Am I right?'

Dan felt dazed—as much by her determination to dissect things he would normally leave unsaid as by her perception. 'Yes, you're absolutely right.'

'Thought so.'

'And just how—out of interest—did you know all that?'

'One of my little brothers was exactly the same—always had to be the one in charge. Your bottom lip looked very similar—he used to stick *his* out when he didn't get his own way!'

Dan felt the irresistible urge to smile at one of the most unflattering things which had ever been said about him. 'I don't think I've ever been compared to somebody's *brother* before,' he mused, wondering just what else this weekend was going to throw up.

And, since they seemed to have strayed into the minefield of home-truths, maybe it was time for one of his own. 'Do you *never* wear make-up, Megan?'

She tilted her chin defensively. 'Sometimes. Not very often.'

'Unusual,' he commented, thinking that when you actually *looked* at her eyes they were the most beautiful green-gold colour.

'Not where I come from. There wasn't much call for it on the farm.' She hoped that she wasn't coming over as some kind of hick. 'And I went without it for so long that I just never got into the habit of wearing it. Now I can't be bothered, most of the time. Certainly not for work.' She threw him an uncertain look. 'Why? Do you think I should?'

'I think it would be interesting to see what it made you look like,' he answered truthfully.

Which made Megan's mind up for her.

Half of her had been wondering whether to ditch much of the advice given to her by her more worldly housemate, but now she could see that Helen might be right.

Dan obviously thought that she needed to change her image for the forthcoming weekend, too. So maybe she would throw caution to the wind, and indulge herself in some of those wild, extravagant clothes which were now at her disposal...

They left straight after work on Friday, which meant that Megan had to do a quick change in the ladies' loo, where she shoe-horned herself into the yellow satin trousers, together with a black silk top of Helen's. It had a low, scoop neck and three-quarter-length sleeves and was actually very flattering. The only thing was that Helen had insisted she buy a new bra to go with it—and it was one of those bras which gave you a cleavage as deep as the Grand Canyon. Immensely flattering,

but rather flamboyant. Still, Jake Haddon
would probably appreciate it!

She brushed her hair and tied it back in her
usual ponytail, then she stepped back and
blinked at her reflection in the mirror.

She certainly looked different! And there
would be plenty of time before dinner to
change into the safe black dress she had
brought with her—if she needed to!

She walked out of the washroom and saw
the telephonist do a double-take and wondered what conclusion she must have come
to, especially since Dan was sitting right outside the building in the car, waiting for her.

She opened the door and gingerly slid one
satin-covered leg onto the passenger seat.
'Dan?'

Dan's pupils dilated as an endlessly slim
and shiny canary-coloured leg swam into his
line of vision. 'What?' He swallowed as a
pert bottom now appeared and perched itself
on the seat beside his.

'Aren't you worried about what people
might think?' she asked him, neatly swinging
her other leg in.

He hadn't been. But maybe now...

'About what?' he asked huskily.

Megan inched her legs as far away from his as possible. Funny how enclosed a car space could suddenly seem. 'About us disappearing together like this.'

'But assistants often accompany their bosses on trips,' he said, hiding a smile as he noticed her edging away from him. 'Sometimes even further than the Cotswolds!'

'Yes, I know, but this is a bit different, isn't it?'

'Well, it's nothing to do with work.' Dan adjusted the driving mirror. 'But I assume that you don't gossip about me and breach the confidentiality of our working relationship?'

'I've told my flat mate, that's all. Presumably that's not breaking the Official Secrets Act?'

He smiled. She looked almost pretty when she was indignant. 'You have such a sarcastic tongue sometimes.'

'That's what one of my brothers always says.'

Another reference to her family. He guessed they had to talk about *something* during the long drive ahead. 'Just how many brothers do you have?'

'Four. I'm the oldest.'

He raised his eyebrows. 'Your mother must have had her work cut out,' he smiled.

Megan cleared her throat. 'Look, this is always very difficult and I don't want you to start going on about how sorry you are, because it happened a long time ago—but my mother actually died in childbirth when I was nine—'

'Oh, my God!' He felt his heart miss a beat as he heard her trying to inject a note of nonchalance into her voice. 'Megan—'

'What I cannot *bear*,' she said fiercely, 'is when people start treating me differently, because of it. So you don't have to suddenly start being nice to me. Okay?'

Dan forced himself to laugh. 'Why? Am I usually so horrible to you, then?'

Megan allowed a smile to creep over her lips. 'No comment!'

'What happened to the baby?' he asked suddenly.

She turned her head to look at him, reluctantly impressed. Most people were too embarrassed to ask. 'The ''baby'' is now sixteen, and wants to be an engineer.'

'Did you look after him all on your own?'

Megan nodded. 'Mostly. My father was always busy on the farm, and the other boys weren't really interested. But I loved it. Or, rather, I loved *him*!'

He thought how lucky her brothers were to have a sister with such generosity of spirit. 'And just so you know, Megan, I do have some idea what it feels like. My father died when I wasn't much older than you were.'

'Oh. I'm sorry,' she said quickly. His words made her feel better and she didn't know why. Or maybe she did. Just for once, it was nice not to feel alone. A sad childhood could sometimes mark you out—make you different. Or, at least, make you *feel* different.

'Now,' he said, in the very definite tone of someone who wanted to change the subject, 'what music would you like to listen to? Or do you prefer the news report?'

'Oh, music,' she said instantly. 'The news is always so *depressing*.'

He laughed softly as he reached out and clicked into a music station playing classical music, which she didn't normally like. But the car was warm and the soft music lulled her and sent her thoughts drifting off some place else. It was a long drive but she must have slept for most of it because, when her eyes began to flicker open again, all that remained of the sun was a distant rose tinge to the horizon.

'So you're awake at last,' observed a soft voice beside her.

Megan started, still feeling groggy. She turned her head a little to see Dan's profile etched against the dying midsummer light and blinked in confusion until she remembered just where she was. Had she been awake all the time, or had she been dreaming about him?

He chose that very moment to slow down, sliding his hand over the gear stick in a way which made her feel even more disorientated than she was already. Her hair was falling all over the place and she was dying for a bath. 'What time is it?' She yawned.

He winced. 'It's getting on for ten and we're late. We were held up by roadworks for ages. I called my brother and spoke to him on the car phone, but even that didn't wake you.' He'd half wished it had. She must have been having some sort of peculiar dream because she had been quietly moaning and squirming her bottom in a way which had made concentrating on the road extremely difficult indeed.

'Was he angry?

'Of course he wasn't angry! But he said they may start dinner without us.' He saw her pull a face. 'Sorry.'

'It can't be helped. Do you suppose I'll have time for a bath?'

He heard the plaintive note in her voice. 'Unlikely,' he offered. 'But don't worry. You look—er—fine as you are!' He found his eyes drawn reluctantly to the slim yellow thighs and looked away again. 'Just fine.'

He turned the car into a sweeping gravel drive which seemed to go on for miles. And it wasn't until a building appeared—glowing golden and pink on the horizon, and looking for all the world like a magical Disney castle—that Megan realised they were here.

CHAPTER FOUR

MEGAN stared at the vast house in astonishment. She'd never seen anywhere quite like it before—except in photos in guide books and history books. Imagine growing up in a place like this! Why hadn't he *warned* her?

Edgewood House was a beautiful and ancient brick building which seemed to rise out of the land as though it had been there for ever. The last rays of the sun had flecked the moat which surrounded it with molten gold and the brickwork was the warm, deep colour of mottled raspberries.

'Oh, my goodness!' said Megan, and sat up in her seat to see better. 'I can't believe it! Is this really where you live?'

'Where I *used* to live,' he corrected.

'How old is it?'

'The north side of the house dates back to Henry VII's time.' He changed down a gear. 'Other wings have been added over the centuries. It isn't particularly uniform, but it works, I think.'

'Oh, yes,' she breathed. 'It certainly does!'

Dan watched the pleasure which had made her body uncurl without inhibition. A lack of inhibition which was only emphasised by those exotic clothes he'd never seen her in before. And, for some extraordinary reason, the breath caught in his throat like dust. 'Like it?'

'*Like* it? I love it! Who wouldn't?' And she added almost wistfully, 'How can something which is so old, glow as richly?'

'You'll have to talk to my brother about that. He says very similar things about the place. It's something to do with how they made the bricks. But Adam will be able to tell you.'

'Is he older or younger than you?'

'Older.' A pause. 'And traditionally the one who'll inherit the house.'

'Gosh. Lucky man!'

'Yes. Isn't he? He's also engaged to be married,' he added evenly. 'Just thought I'd let you know.'

His suave observation didn't fool her for a minute. Megan knew exactly what he was getting at! 'Can't I make an innocent comment without it being misconstrued?' she asked him heatedly. 'Do you think I'm about to make a play for your brother simply because I like the house?'

'Since you ask, some women *do* see the house and imagine themselves as the mistress of it,' he agreed coolly. 'But you're right—it was an assumption I had no right to make about you.' He pulled the key out of the ignition and shifted in his seat as he turned to face her.

'When you grow up in a place as beautiful as this, you soon become suspicious of people's motives. People just see the trappings, and not the person beneath those trappings.'

'Poor little rich boy!' she mocked softly. 'Is that why you've never married—because you've never found a woman whose motives you don't suspect?'

The question took him off guard. And its implication made him feel very slightly foolish. People rarely asked him outright, and certainly not as bluntly as that, even though he suspected that they wondered often enough.

'You're a very bold woman, Megan Phillips.'

'Ah, I'm told I'm often rather blunt—sorry.' She smiled. 'Don't worry; you aren't on the witness stand, Dan. You can always refuse to answer, you know!'

'But you told me I was to answer all your questions this weekend,' he retorted mockingly. 'I've never married because I've never found anyone I wanted to marry. Simple as that.'

'But there must have been a good few—' Megan bit her lip as she struggled to find the right word '—contenders!' she finished triumphantly.

'We're not talking about a boxing match!'

'So you've never even come close to it?'

'Never.' He gave a wry smile. 'And you?'

She thought about David. 'Not really,' she admitted.

'Don't look so tragic, Megan—it's not the end of the world. Marriage is a vastly overrated institution, you know. Look at all the fall-out and casualties if you don't believe me.'

'But surely you want a family of your own one day?' she persisted. 'A little boy who looks just like you, before you're too old to kick a ball around with him?'

For a moment there was a long and dis-believing silence. If it had been anyone else, in any other circumstances… Dan thought he might eject her from the car there and then for her audacity. But right now he needed her—and need, he was fast discovering, made you vulnerable in all kinds of unexpected ways.

'I can still just about manage to connect my foot with a ball,' he commented acidly. 'And I hope to continue being active for as long as possible!' He breathed a sigh of relief as he saw the front door open, and his brother appeared.

'Here's Adam now,' he added. 'My big brother.'

Except that he was smaller, thought Megan as she tugged down the black top over her hips.

Adam didn't look any older than Dan and his build was lighter. Which did not mean he wasn't an attractive man. Because he was. Exceedingly attractive, in fact, thought Megan as she climbed out of the car to greet him.

It was just that she was fast discovering that Dan was something else; she was seeing him in an entirely different light...

At work he was simply different because he didn't slob around in jeans and trainers, like most of the other men at Softshare. His beautifully cut suits always seemed more of an idiosyncrasy than any kind of fashion statement.

But here he seemed to blend in perfectly with the imposing house and stunning gardens.

The dark gleam of his hair and the proud, aquiline profile could easily have come from another century—but the lazy smile and the glint in his eyes were unashamedly modern. He looked more Lord of the Manor than his brother did—and Megan wondered whether there had ever been any resentment between the siblings over who would inherit.

Adam turned towards her with a curious smile.

'This is Megan,' said Dan. 'Megan Phillips. Remember—I told you I was bringing someone with me.'

'Yes, I know you did, but I couldn't quite believe it until I had seen it with my own eyes!'

Adam held his hand out, but not before Megan had seen the fleeting look of surprise in his eyes, so swift that she might almost have imagined it. Except that she hadn't imagined it, and she had a very good idea about its source. She supposed that whenever Dan brought girls here they looked like the type of person who would feel and look at home in such a magnificent setting.

Not personal assistants who had come straight from work wearing borrowed clothes!

'I'm very pleased to meet you, Megan,' said Adam, his accent almost identical to his brother's. 'I must say, Dan's been keeping you very quiet!.'

'And you can see why, can't you?' questioned Dan warmly, putting his arm around Megan's shoulder and giving it a little squeeze. 'She's gorgeous, isn't she?'

Megan tipped her face upwards and hoped that he saw the light of warning which glittered from her eyes. It said: please don't overdo the affection bit. Particularly when she'd never felt less gorgeous in her life! But, annoyingly, he left his arm exactly where it was—resting across her back in that casual yet affectionate way which was curiously easy.

And toe-curlingly moreish.

'Gorgeous!' agreed Adam politely.

'Lovely to meet you,' Megan smiled back, and, seeing as he didn't appear about to remove it himself, she shook Dan's arm away with a wriggle of her shoulder. 'Not now, darling!' she said firmly.

'Ah!' Adam's eyes glinted. 'That explains it, then!'

'Explains what?' asked Dan.

'What this woman has to make you bring her home!' Adam winked hugely at Megan. 'I've been out with him many times, and he usually has to fight them off—so a woman pushing him away is obviously just what our Dan needs! Come on in, Megan, and welcome...'

They followed him inside and Megan was taken aback by the sheer beauty and dimensions of the entrance hall, where a magnificent carved staircase curved up to the first floor, before it branched into two. She craned her neck to get a better look.

Why hadn't he told her that his 'home' was almost as big as a castle? Why, any minute now and a party of tourists would probably appear from behind a pillar!

'Now,' said Adam. 'Do you want the good news or the bad news?'

Dan grimaced. 'Go on.'

'Well, earlier in the week Mother was called away to the sickbed of an old school-friend,' Adam explained. 'The hypochondri-acal one. You know—gets a twinge and calls out the paramedics.'

'It beats me why Mother always rushes to her side,' sighed Dan.

'Who knows?' shrugged Adam. 'Any-way—the situation has now been reversed. Yesterday, Mother managed to break her an-kle and the friend is looking after *her*. What's more, the doctor has told her it would be bet-ter not to travel until early next week.' He paused and grinned. 'So I've put you both in the same room.'

Megan stiffened in horror. 'But that's ab-solutely—'

'The most wonderful piece of news I've heard all week—I absolutely agree with you, my darling,' purred Dan, and he pulled Megan into his arms and began to kiss her, right in front of his brother!

Megan had been opening her mouth to protest about sharing a room, but her protest turned into something quite different. His kiss was the very last thing she had been expecting, and its effect on her was even more shocking than the fact that Dan didn't seem to care that they had an audience!

Or that the audience was staring at the two of them in a kind of disbelieving wonder.

Megan's open mouth had given Dan immediate intimate access—which she was horrified to discover that he was taking full advantage of! There was no hesitation as his lips fused against hers and he slicked his tongue inside her mouth with masterful assurance, making her feel weak and tiny and fragile.

And somehow—stupidly—she found that she couldn't resist him. So that, instead of pushing him away, her hands slipped up to his shoulders—almost without her noticing they had done so!

Megan felt her eyelids fluttering to a close and her fingernails curling like a kitten's around his neck. She found that she wanted more than anything in the world to wind her arms sinuously around his neck and to press her body blatantly close to his and to...

There came the sound of a polite cough, and Megan's eyes snapped open and for a moment she was lost in a grey gaze so stormy that she couldn't decide whether Dan was as stunned and confused and turned on by that kiss as she was.

Probably not. He'd probably kissed more people in a week than she had in a lifetime.

Dan stared back at her as the dull thunder in his heart subsided. He'd kissed her mainly out of mischief. Inspired by that look of sheer horror on her face when Adam had told her they were sharing. Most women would have leapt at the chance, not looked as if they'd just been sentenced to twenty years' hard labour!

At least, that was how it had started.

So what had happened *next*?

He thought how typical it was that the unexpected could so often outshine what was carefully planned. Like how a meal thrown together out of all the odd things you had knocking around the kitchen could sometimes taste a million times better than the expensive restaurant you had to book for.

And so it was with Megan and that kiss. He had taken her off guard and her genuine surprise had been sweet. Very sweet. More than sweet—she had stirred the blood in his veins and left him feeling... Dan swallowed. Left him feeling very, very aroused indeed...

With a start, he realised that Adam was talking to them and that his words had been skimming past his ears unheard.

'Er, sorry to break things up,' grinned Adam, looking at his brother with something very much like amazement. 'But I can always shoot back into the dining room and come back in ten minutes, if you two can't bear to keep your hands off each other!'

Megan brought the tips of her fingers up to cool her flaming cheeks, praying that Dan wouldn't say anything to his brother which would only make matters worse.

'Oh, we'll have plenty of time for love-making later,' murmured Dan, thoroughly enjoying the daggers which were glinting from her eyes. 'So run along and wash your face, sweetheart. The cloakroom's over there.' He pointed. 'I'll wait here with Adam.'

Fuming, Megan virtually bolted off in the direction of the cloakroom, silently uttering every curse she knew. Her hands was shaking as she filled the huge, old-fashioned sink with cold water—though whether it was with rage or frustration she couldn't quite decide.

What on earth had he done *that* for?

And why had she responded with the enthusiasm of a woman who had never been kissed before?

She looked in the mirror and turned her mouth down at the corners.

What a sight!

Her lips seemed much darker than usual, her cheeks were all flushed and her eyes were glittering like stars. Dan had managed to do all that to her just by kissing her—and it hadn't even been a proper kiss.

Just a very effective way of shutting her up!

She washed her hands and face and pulled the band out of her hair while she brushed it and left it hanging down over her shoulders. Not the most exciting style in the world, but at least it hid some of her face.

Then she took a deep breath and walked back out into the hall where Dan was waiting with his brother—looking for all the world as though he had just heard the most wonderful joke but was keeping it all to himself!

She met his amused stare with a furious look, and she didn't care if his brother saw it or not. *Just you wait,* her eyes said menacingly.

Mmm! Should be fun! came back the silent and teasing response.

Adam was looking from Megan to his brother in bemusement. 'I must say, I've never seen my brother display such an uninhibited passion before,' he smiled. 'What have you done to him, Megan?'

'I just couldn't resist her,' sighed Dan.

Oh, if only Adam knew that this was all an act, thought Megan. How disappointed he would be!

The walk along an echoing corridor towards the dining room felt like a long walk to the gallows and Megan had to remind herself that she was here doing Dan a favour—not the other way round. And she would tell him that just as soon as she got the opportunity—along with a threat to leave if there

was going to be any repeat of that outrageously sexy behaviour.

The murmur of voices and the muffled
chinking of glasses told her they were close,
and Adam flung open the double doors with
a dramatic gesture, to announce, 'Ladies and
gentlemen—at last, our late but very welcome arrivals! My brother Dan and…Miss
Megan Phillips!'

A sea of curious faces swam in front of
her, far too many to take in all at once.
Megan took a deep breath to steady her
nerves as she slowly became aware of fine
crystal and china, a chandelier which
gleamed as brightly as the moon in a desert
sky and five pairs of curious eyes fixed solely
on *her*!

And no wonder—all three women were in
smooth, sleek dresses, while she looked as if
she had just escaped from the circus in her
yellow satin trousers!

'Well, well, well,' came a bluff greeting
from an older man who sat at the far end of
the tennis-court-sized table. 'It's young
McKnight with a woman on his arm. Well,
they say there's a first time for everything—
so it must be serious!'

'Please don't say things like that, Colonel!' joked Dan. 'Or you'll frighten Megan away!'

Now that all the eyes had fixed on Dan, Megan could allow herself to stare as she tried to work out who was who.

There was a plump, middle-aged woman with enough gems around her neck to rival the glittering chandelier. She was probably married to the colonel, Megan thought.

A couple of places along was a slim young woman in a simple red silk dress, with short hair the colour of butter and elegant features. The glittering sapphire on the third finger of her left hand made her the most likely candidate to be Adam's fiancée.

Next to her was a young man who appeared to be in his mid-twenties—maybe the same age as Megan herself, though he looked much younger, she decided. And a positive *schoolboy* if you stood him next to Dan.

And that must be Katrina, Megan thought, looking at the girl who was gazing at Dan as though all her birthdays had arrived at once. She was fresh-faced and sparkly-eyed beautiful. And so terribly, terribly *young*.

Dan touched Megan's elbow with the palm of his hand and she was startled by the effect that the light, brushing gesture had on her. Electric. And yet curiously comfortable. As though it was the most natural thing in the world for him to be touching her.

'Let me introduce you,' he said, eyes crinkling in a relaxed way that Megan wasn't used to seeing. 'The beauty in the red dress is soon to become my sister-in-law. This is Megan, Amanda!'

Amanda winked at Megan. 'When I started seeing Adam, I didn't realise that he had such a silver-tongued younger brother! Nice to meet you, Megan.'

'Nice to meet you too,' smiled Megan.

'And Colonel Maddison you've just met—' Dan continued.

'Charles!' corrected the colonel, with a twinkle in his eye. 'I'm retired from the army now, Dan—and I can't be doing with the old hierarchy!'

Dan smiled at the woman sporting the costly gems. 'His wife, Ruth.'

'Hello,' said Megan politely.

'And this is my mother's god-daughter— Katrina Hobkirk.'

It was a very detached way to describe someone, Megan thought as she heard

Katrina suck her breath into her lungs in a shudder. And there was something almost painful in the sudden stiffening of her beautiful, young body as she stared at Dan in hopeless adoration.

And what Megan had *not* been expecting was that Katrina should be so very beautiful. Like a madonna—except that her innocent air was tempered with a very obvious look of the predator about her. And that look was directed very firmly at Dan.

She was wearing what was obviously a very expensive black dress which was much too old for her. Her black hair hung in a cloud around her shoulders and her face was so pale that it looked completely white in contrast.

But it was those doe-brown eyes which were fixed with such unwavering adoration on Dan's face which were a complete giveaway. Even the most insensitive person could have read the emotion in her face. No wonder the atmosphere round the table was far from easy.

And if bringing Megan here was supposed to have been an effective deterrent against a schoolgirl crush, then—so far at least—it wasn't working.

'Hello, Dan,' Katrina said breathily.

'Hello, Katrina,' he smiled gently. 'Say hello to Megan.'

The doe eyes were not so luminous nor so loving now. They flickered briefly as they took in the unmade-up face and her vivid trousers and low-cut top. Megan's already shaky ego received another battering as she witnessed herself being mentally dismissed.

And it was the most insulting experience!

Katrina slanted Dan a surprised look, as if to say, Why *her*? 'Hello, Megan,' she said politely. Then, with protocol out of the way, she continued to devour Dan with her eyes. 'How are you, Dan? I haven't seen you for ages and you haven't answered any of my letters, either! Come and sit down! See—I've saved a seat for you beside me.'

Megan found herself briefly lanced by a sharp grey gaze, which seemed to say, *See what I mean?*

And yes, she did.

Adoration that went as deep as Katrina's for Dan was difficult to shift. Because when someone was in the throes of an infatuation that intense, then that person saw only what they wanted to see. And Katrina clearly had no difficulty confusing Dan's affection for loving.

Megan decided to stop acting as though her tongue had been removed! She sat down and turned to the forgotten young man at her side, and smiled.

'And who are you?' she asked softly.

His beam of gratitude seemed a little out of proportion, considering that all she had done was say hello to him.

'I'm Neil Baron, another friend of the family—I was invited at the last minute probably because the numbers weren't even,' he said self-deprecatingly. 'Nice to meet you, Megan. Oh, and congratulations!'

Megan leaned back in her seat while Dan took the empty place between her and Katrina. 'What for?'

'For managing to nail the last great bachelor, of course!'

'Oh, but it's not a bit like that!' put in Megan hurriedly as her glass was filled with white wine.

'Like what?' queried Neil.

'Well, we're certainly not engaged or any-thing!'

'No, we're not, are we, darling?' came a lazy drawl of agreement from her right-hand side, and Megan turned her head to find a cool and speculative gaze fixed on her.

And he seemed to leave the words 'not yet' hanging unspoken in the air.

Megan thought to herself that if Dan hadn't chosen computers as his profession, then he would have done very well as an ac-tor, with a performance like that! Maybe she was about to see an entirely different side of her boss this weekend.

Katrina *did* take notice of Megan then. She gave a smile which was obviously forced and it was accompanied by the glitter of combat in those huge brown eyes. 'I should think not,' she said prettily. 'Because if Dan went away and got engaged without telling us we would all be very angry indeed!' She gave him a little side smile. 'Especially if it was to someone we didn't know.'

There was an uneasy laugh of agreement around the table, and then a woman who was obviously some kind of housekeeper appeared, carrying two extra plates of food, and Megan began to brighten.

She was *starving*!

'Like some more wine?' asked Neil.

'Yes, please.' Megan held her glass out. 'If ever I needed a drink, it's tonight!'

Neil smiled. 'Why, is it such a terrifying prospect, meeting Dan's family?

'Yes, it's terrifying,' she agreed.

'He keeps staring at you when he doesn't think you're looking,' confided Neil.

Yes. She'd noticed that herself—and she was going to have to talk to Dan about that. She'd never had him down as the adoring type, and she doubted whether anyone else had, either. And if he overplayed the role too much, then surely they risked being found out?

Out of the corner of his eye, Dan saw her eating as though she was famished. Maybe she was. His own appetite seemed to have waned and he couldn't work out why. He was listening to Katrina and trying to appear interested in what she had to say, without sending out any kind of message that he was *too* interested.

He sighed. It was a pretty complicated situation all round. And so far, at least, Katrina didn't seem to see Megan as any kind of threat. But maybe that wasn't so very surprising.

He glanced over at where Megan was giggling at something Neil was saying, while Neil was looking absolutely delighted that someone found him amusing enough to laugh at his jokes.

Dan frowned. She didn't look at her best tonight, that was for sure—but she looked better than he had ever seen her. The trousers were a little loud, it was true, but a definite improvement on her usual dreary clothes.

He'd never seen a woman at a dinner table who had taken less effort with her appearance, and yet he found himself admiring the way she sat there, chatting so animatedly. As if, yes, she would have preferred to have changed—but that in the grand scheme of things she wasn't going to let it trouble her too much.

And besides, wasn't that the whole point of this charade? To prove to Katrina that love was unpredictable where it struck—and not just a series of numbers you clicked in, and then waited for the jackpot to come up?

Dan frowned. Just because Katrina was young and beautiful, with the same kind of background as his own, that did not mean that he and she were automatically a match made in heaven. However much she wanted it.

'Megan?' He touched Megan's forearm with the tip of one finger, slightly alarmed when she slammed her wineglass down on the table in response. Through the sensitive nerve-endings of his finger, he could feel the tiny hairs on her skin as minute goosebumps began to spring up in response.

His mouth hardened. What kind of reaction was that, for heaven's sake? He'd brought her here partly because she *didn't* find him attractive—so why was her body suddenly acting as if she did?

He stared at her. In the candlelight, her hazel eyes gleamed like a cat's, but the faint hints of green and gold gave them a curiously exotic appearance. She was the only woman in the room not wearing any make-up and he thought how healthy and fresh her skin looked. She smelt of soap...clean and pure and innocent.

Megan frowned at him. Why was he touching her arm? And why was he staring at her like that? Surely drawing attention to the fact that every other woman in the room must have spent hours in the bathroom getting ready to come down to dinner that night— while she had been sitting fast asleep in a traffic jam!

She bit back a yawn. She'd dutifully chatted to everyone around the table and enjoyed it—especially talking to Adam and Amanda, a couple who somehow managed to be madly in love without excluding the rest of the world from their conversation.

But now the long day had caught up with her and she was dying to get to bed. But even that wasn't going to be easy, in view of who she was going to be sharing a room with.

'Yes, Dan, what is it?' she asked, more impatiently than she had intended, and found herself trapped in the snare of his eyes.

And something happened.

Something so nebulous that Megan couldn't have defined it if she'd tried—and afterwards half wondered whether she had imagined it. An awareness—no more than that. A realisation that maybe she hadn't been completely honest with herself.

Had she told him that she didn't find him attractive? Then she had either been lying or deluding herself.

Because, right then, he looked like the most gorgeous man she had ever seen—his hair gleaming in the candlelight, his smile lazy, that elegant, long-limbed body leaning back against his chair as he looked at her with narrow-eyed interest.

Dan saw Megan's lips part, and whatever he had been planning to say flew clean out of his head. For a split second they stared at each other with something approaching disbelief. Almost as if... Dan frowned.

'Is something wrong?' she demanded.

He shook his head to clear it. 'I was going to ask you the same question. You looked, I don't know...jumpy.'

'Are you surprised?' she quizzed in an undertone. 'I feel as if I'm—'

'Dan?'

Katrina was tugging insistently on his jacket sleeve, like a child demanding an ice-cream.

He resisted a sigh. 'Yes, Katrina?' He turned to look down into the heart-shaped face which was raised so earnestly to his.

It had been almost a year since he had seen her, and in that time she had grown very beautiful, he realised. No longer a child, nor a girl—but now a fully fledged woman with needs of her own and no shyness about expressing them.

And surely that made the need for this slightly ridiculous charade he had concocted with Megan all the more necessary.

For it was becoming obvious, at least to him, that if Katrina continued with this fixation, then she risked making a complete fool of herself.

And the ego was fragile at her age, he reminded himself. A decade on and she would shrug off rejection with the thought that life was short and memories even shorter. But right now she was a vulnerable and volatile age…

'Can I have some of your chocolate mousse?' Katrina asked him.

He looked down at his dish, and then at the moist lips she was presenting to him, and realised that she wanted to share the spoon, or for him to feed her. Eating as a substitute for sex, he thought grimly. Well, tough. He certainly wasn't going to play *that* game.

'Help yourself,' he smiled pleasantly, and pushed the bowl towards her.

'Oh,' pouted Katrina. 'Don't you want to spoon-feed me, Dan?'

'You're a big girl now,' he said lightly. 'You can feed yourself.'

Megan was watching exactly what was going on between them, though she was still managing to keep part of her attention on the long and rather boring story of how Neil should have been born in America, but wasn't.

She ate the last spoonful of cream and pushed the bowl away, thinking that Katrina wasn't *quite* as sweet or as innocent as she had imagined. And Katrina's obsession went deeper than she had thought.

Dan had been right. It was becoming more than just a crush, or an overgrown infatuation. There was the sense that behind the beautiful façade lay a kind of wild desperation. How far, she wondered, would Katrina go to get what she wanted?

'You looked bushed,' came a soft voice from beside her.

'That's because I am.'

'Want to go to bed?'

The warmth and intimacy of the question made Megan flounder around for a suitable reply. Because when he spoke to her like that it made it a little easier for her to understand what Katrina might be feeling.

Charles Maddison must have heard it too, for he laughed from the other end of the dining-room table. 'Oh, for heaven's sake, Dan—can't you at least wait until after the port?'

Dan rose to his feet, placing his hand on the back of Megan's neck and feeling tension knotted in the muscles there. 'No, I think I'll skip the port and call it a night. Megan and I have been working since very early this morning—'

'I'll *bet* you have!' chuckled Charles enviously, until his wife glared and elbowed him in the ribs.

Katrina looked as if someone had just flesh-wounded her. 'You're going to *bed*?'

Dan steeled himself against the hurt and appeal in her eyes. 'Yes, we are. We'll see you all tomorrow morning.' He saw her wince at the proprietorial 'we' and he felt a pang of regret that she needed to be hurt this way. But what alternative did he have? 'Come on, Megan,' he instructed softly.

Megan allowed him to pull her chair back and to stand attentively by her side while they said goodnight, and then, to the sound of deafening silence, Dan looped his arm over her shoulder with all the possessiveness of a real lover as they left the dining room together.

CHAPTER FIVE

MEGAN forced herself to bite her tongue as she followed Dan along the portrait-strewn corridor to the great hall. She had plenty she wanted to say to him, but she didn't want the others to hear.

And she couldn't see her luggage any-where!

She turned to him. 'Where's my suitcase?'

'Upstairs.' He met her belligerent gaze with an enquiring look. 'In your room.'

'Huh! Don't you mean *our* room? Funny, I don't remember that being part of the deal!'

In the distance came the sound of chairs being scraped back against the floor.

Dan scowled. 'Come on, Megan. Let's go upstairs!'

'Let's not,' she argued. 'At least, not until we've sorted out the sleeping arrangements to our *mutual satisfaction.*'

Snippets of conversation wafted down the corridor from the direction of the dining room.

'Obviously, I can understand your concern,' he growled.

'How very perceptive of you!'

'But I don't want to have to conduct this *particular* conversation with an attentive audience listening to every word we say.'

Her eyes challenged him. 'I'll bet you don't!'

He drew a breath, as if trying to remind himself to remain calm. 'Megan,' he said softly, 'if the whole point of your being here is to maintain some kind of illusion of being in love with me—'

'Yes,' she agreed, wondering now whether she'd been completely mad to go along with it.

'Then won't it rather give the game away if we're caught sparring about who sleeps where?'

'Not necessarily. I might be the kind of woman who jealously guards her virtue,' said Megan piously. 'Mightn't I?

Dan's eyes gleamed with possibility. 'So you might. But then, surely you would be struggling with your conscience, and not your outrage?'

Megan stared at him uncomprehendingly.

'So why don't you save the disgust you're obviously feeling until we get upstairs?' he explained tightly. 'And let's go there right now. Before Katrina gets the chance to wonder why you're looking so horrified at the thought of spending the night with me!'

He did have a point, Megan conceded—and there seemed little left to do other than to follow him up the grand staircase.

It was difficult not to be impressed. She imagined the different women who must have mounted these same stairs over the centuries, with their silken dresses and lace petticoats elegantly brushing the ground as they walked. And here *she* was among their company—in garish yellow trousers and rubber-soled shoes!

A large bronze bust of a young boy sat on a marble plinth when they reached the top. If it had been anywhere else it might have looked ridiculous, but in this great, high-ceilinged place it fitted in perfectly.

Megan paused in front of it, certain that she recognised a certain stubborn tilt of the chin. And wasn't there something awfully familiar about that aqualine nose? And the thickly lashed eyes? 'Who *is* that?'

He looked at her suspiciously. 'It's me.'

'I thought it was.' She smiled, thinking how awful it must have been for a boy of that age to sit still long enough to have a bust made of him. 'What a pretty boy you were, Dan!'

He hadn't been teased like that for years. Or, at least, not in that sunny, innocent way. Dan only knew teasing as part of sexual fore-play. And it was glaringly obvious from Megan's body language that sex was the last thing on her mind as she ran her finger down over the marble nose as if she was searching for dust!

He should have felt insulted by her indif-ference, and yet he did not. Instead, Dan felt a kick of unrecognisable emotion somewhere deep in his gut and sensed a sudden, un-known danger in the air.

'This way,' he growled softly, jabbing his finger towards the left-hand corridor. 'This is where we're sleeping.'

Megan screwed up her eyes as she tramped past yet more family portraits and then turned sharply left down another corridor. This place was like a maze! He stopped in front of a heavily panelled door and she realised that they were here.

Dan heard her breath catch and quicken and his own heart began to thunder as he pushed the door open. He felt the powerful white heat of desire and shook his head in despair and disbelief. This was crazy! None of this was real—he'd asked Megan to take part because he *didn't* find her attractive. So why the sudden eye-lock at dinner? And the subsequent lingering awareness?

'This is our room,' he announced woodenly.

'So I see,' said Megan, feeling as nervous as a virgin bride on her honeymoon.

But her nerves were put on hold when she saw what awaited her. Because the bedroom, like the house, was something completely outside Megan's experience. And, for a moment at least, she forgot all about the night ahead, she was so awestruck by the beauty in front of her.

The room was dominated by a massive four-poster bed, hung with drapes of golden silk and deepest green velvet. Each wall was completely covered with tapestries—which seemed to depict a lot of plump women in see-through dresses playing various musical instruments, or holding bunches of grapes.

'This isn't your old bedroom, is it?' she gasped.

'You're kidding!' He started laughing as he pushed the door closed. 'We children weren't supposed to come anywhere near this wing. No, this is the Green Velvet Room— named after the hangings around the bed.'

'Oh, great!' Megan pulled a face. 'A room named after a bed! That's *just* what I needed!' And it put paid to any hope that she might be able to forget about that monstrous great pale green mattress as it gleamed with quiet threat in the centre of the room.

Agitatedly Megan walked over to the window and peered out into the darkened night. All she could make out were the scarecrow shadows of the trees and the gleam of silver as moonlight was reflected off the moat. She waited until she felt calmer before turning to face him again. 'You know, this isn't exactly working out as I expected, Dan.'

'I know.'

She wondered how he had the nerve to give her that cool look of resignation.

'Why didn't you object when your brother told you we were sharing a bedroom?'

'And say what?' he demanded. 'That we didn't want to? That we were waiting until we were married?'

'Why not?' she challenged.

'Because Adam wouldn't have believed me,' he answered simply.

'Oh, wouldn't he?' Megan fixed him with a challenging stare. 'Does that mean that every woman you date you have sex with?'

'Don't be naive. What the hell do *you* think?' He gave a brief, hard smile as he heard the disapproval which laced her words. 'But I don't date that many,' he added softly as he saw the disapproval turn into outrage.

'It's nothing to do with me if you sleep with every woman on the planet!'

'Naturally, Adam would expect us to share a room,' he told her gently. 'And maybe he should have checked first—but he probably wasn't sure *what* to do. You see, I've never brought a woman back here before.'

Megan's mouth gaped open. 'What— *never*?'

'No. Never,' he echoed, smiling at the look of astonishment on her face.

'Why not?'

He sighed. 'Because it's my family home, and because it's special. I told you...women get dollar signs lighting up their eyes when they see a place like this. Why would I bring someone here, if it only gave them a false impression of how much they meant to me?'

'I guess so,' she agreed slowly.

'My brother has obviously made a perfectly natural assumption about how important you must be to me. If I tell him that we're simply—'

'Just good friends?' she filled in sarcastically.

He *had* been about to say 'friends', but realised that they didn't qualify as friends at all. They were colleagues. But that didn't seem the right description either. 'If I tell him you work for me and that our so-called "relationship" doesn't exist, then it will show in his attitude towards you. It's bound to. Adam isn't the world's greatest actor—'

'Unlike his brother, you mean?'

'What are you getting at, Megan?'

'Think about it!'

'I am.'

'Then don't give me that wide-eyed look of innocence. I'm talking about that kiss.'

'What was wrong with it?'

'You know very well that nothing was *wrong* with it!'

Dan smiled. 'Thank heavens for that! For a minute there I thought my technique might be slipping—and that you were complaining!'

'I *was* complaining—'

'Not at the time, you weren't!'

'Well, I am now!' She lifted her hands up in frustration. 'What did you have to go and kiss me like that for?'

'I should think it was perfectly obvious, if you stopped to think about it. You were about to open your mouth and blurt out how appalled you were at the prospect of us being in the same room. And that would have completely given the game away, wouldn't it?'

When he put it like that, it seemed unreasonable not to agree with him. 'Maybe.'

'So. We kissed and we enjoyed it—' He saw her begin to protest and shook his head. 'Yes, we did, Megan. So let's just call it method acting that went a little further than we intended, and forget it ever happened.'

But he had to concentrate to stop a note of husky suggestion from deepening his voice, which he told himself was nothing more than instinct.

And just because the kiss had been a pretty amazing kiss—well, that didn't mean a thing, either. He'd probably only got such a kick out of it because it had been unexpected. And so forbidden. 'Anyway, you'd better have the bed,' he said abruptly. 'And I'll sleep over there by the window.'

Megan looked to where he was pointing— at a faded jade-green chaise longue which, although very beautiful, did not look in the least bit comfortable. And, to be honest, it didn't even look long enough to accommodate Dan's six-foot-plus frame. She sighed. 'Don't be silly. You can share the bed with me.'

Dan's eyes darkened as fantasy sprang to life in his mind and, rather more unfortunately, in his body, too. So much so that he had to shift his position, in case she noticed.

Megan frowned. 'Just don't get carried away with the idea, Dan!'

'What the hell do you expect when you come out with a suggestion like that?' he retorted.

'When I said share the bed, I meant on it—not in it. Or rather I'll be *in* it—you can lie on top of the mattress.'

'Fully clothed, no doubt?' he put in sarcastically.

'That's up to you. You can wear pyjamas, if you'd prefer,' she told him kindly.

'I never wear pyjamas!' he said, in a voice which was as close as he came to snarling.

'Well, then it looks like the first option, doesn't it? There's bound to be a box of blankets somewhere. And why are you looking so shocked?'

He wasn't sure. She certainly wasn't predictable. 'I just thought you'd want me as far away from you as possible, that's all. Especially after all the shock-horror about the kiss!'

'Perhaps you're wondering how I can trust myself to be so close to a man like you, without wanting to leap on top of you in the middle of the night?' she asked him seriously.

'Megan!' He tried to imagine other women in this same situation. And couldn't. They would have played a game. They would have insisted he start out on the chaise longue in the full and certain knowledge of where he would end his night...

Simple.

Whereas nothing seemed to be that straightforward with Megan. Or so simple.

Now he *did* look shocked! Megan smiled. Growing up in a house full of men meant that she didn't have any hang-ups about seeing members of the opposite sex as friends. But clearly Dan did. 'Haven't you ever been to music festivals and shared tents?' she queried. 'Or shared flats with members of the opposite sex? Or fallen asleep at late-night parties?'

'Actually, no.' He frowned. 'I tend to go home when I'm tired.'

'Oh!' Megan raised her eyebrows and hid a smile. 'What a very boring life you must have led, Mr McKnight!'

'Boring?' He suddenly noticed that the tables had turned and that *he* was the one coming over as a prude now! 'No, never boring,' he disagreed softly. 'But never quite as stimulating as it is right at this moment.'

Suddenly her bravado began to evaporate and Megan felt an urgent need to change the subject. 'Er, Dan—'

He had begun to remove his jacket. 'Mmm?'

She wondered nervously whether he was intending to do a full striptease in front of her. 'About Katrina—'

'I know. You see what I mean?' He loosened his tie. 'I just wish she'd get over it.'

'She isn't showing much sign of getting over it.'

'No,' he agreed. 'Which kind of validates you being here.' The grey eyes suddenly hardened. 'You think I encouraged her?'

Megan shook her head. That had honestly never occurred to her. 'No, I don't. Only a man with poor self-esteem would encourage an infatuation he was unable to return.' She paused. 'And I've never noticed you having any problems with *that*.'

He smiled. 'Should I take that as a compliment?'

'No. Just as fact!'

Their gazes locked, and the enormous room suddenly seemed very small. Too small. And there was still the night to get through...

'Where's the bathroom?' she croaked.

Dan was having trouble remembering why he was here in the first place and her words sounded as unfamiliar to his ears as a foreign language might. 'The bathroom?' he repeated.

'The *en suite*?' she elaborated.

At least her innocent comment made him laugh and took some of the edge off the atmosphere. 'You obviously know nothing about the plumbing in these big old houses. There *is* no *en suite*—just a bathroom along the corridor; turn right outside the door and it's the fourth door on the left. And you may find it occupied.'

No en-suite? A queue for the bathroom? How amazing, thought Megan, when these days even the cheapest hotels were fitted with adjoining bathrooms. Maybe the rich really *were* different.

'Right.' She fished around in her overnight bag and pulled some nightclothes out of her suitcase and gave him a brisk smile. 'I'll see you later.' Her smile faltered as her nerve failed her. 'I...er...I expect you'll be asleep by the time I get back.'

'I expect I will,' he agreed gravely, but found her mixture of bravado and nervousness oddly appealing.

He watched her walk out of the room, her head held high, and he was smiling as he poured himself a glass of water from the crystal decanter.

The bathroom was like nothing Megan had ever seen. It was the size of an aircraft hangar, with a huge, free-standing bath, a washbasin you could have swum ducks in and a cistern which sounded like Niagara Falls on a particularly noisy day. But the water was boiling hot and plentiful.

She filled the bath almost to the brim, delighted to be able to strip her clothes off and submerge herself beneath bubbles which smelt subtly of jasmine and tuberose.

For a while she just lay and soaked in the scented water, until all the tension had left her body, and then she washed her hair and brushed her teeth and put on her pyjamas.

She tiptoed back along to the room, half afraid that she might bump into someone. Like Katrina. Or, worse still, the colonel.

What should she do, if she did? Pin a greedy smile of expectation to her mouth as she rushed back to where Dan lay supposedly waiting for a night of wild sex?

She doubted whether she would be able to. Perhaps, like his brother, she was not that good an actor. But fortunately, she arrived back at the room without meeting anyone.

She silently turned the door handle and pushed open the door, her heart sinking when she saw that the lights were still on, and that Dan was just finishing hanging up clothes in one of the wardrobes. It seemed oddly intimate, that simple, unthreatening act of unpacking—somehow even more intimate than sharing a room did.

She would do hers in the morning.

'Oh, you're still awake,' she observed coolly, dumping her clothes and soap-bag on the nearest chair and noticing that he had managed to find a soft pile of blankets from somewhere.

'Well, I thought it a little melodramatic if I just crept onto the bed and—' Dan turned around and his eyes went first very wide, and then very narrow. He made a muffled sound which was somewhere between a plea and a protest. 'Good grief!' he exclaimed softly, staring at her as if he had never seen a woman in her nightwear before.

Megan looked down at herself in confusion. Crisp white cotton pyjamas were hardly the kind of nightwear to inspire any kind of reaction other than bland indifference, surely? Especially when the most daring thing about them was the tiny pink rosebuds embroidered around the demure little Peter Pan collar! 'What's the matter?' she asked.

'I suppose you're going to tell me you're a virgin next?' he groaned aloud, thinking that she looked almost beautiful.

Megan slammed her soap-bag down on the dressing table. 'There has to be a reason why you should come out and ask me an outrageous question like that.'

'Crisp white cotton and a clear, scrubbed face might have something to do with it,' he responded drily. 'I'm surprised you didn't put your hair in pigtails and skip back in singing, "Daddy Wouldn't Buy Me a Bow-Wow".'

'I can if you like!' she responded with bright sarcasm. 'Or would you prefer me to slip into the slinky black satin number I've brought as an alternative?'

'No, I wouldn't!' he groaned again, until he saw the laughter in her eyes. 'You're kidding me?'

Megan smiled. 'Yes, I'm kidding you! Just how many pairs of pyjamas do *you* take away for two nights, Dan?'

'Like I said, I never wear pyjamas,' he answered softly, and held her gaze with a question. 'So. In light of our agreed honesty for the duration of this weekend, are you?'

She was surprised that he had the audacity to ask her again. And yet she found herself admiring his frankness rather than resenting it. 'A virgin?' she questioned coolly. 'I'm twenty-five, for heaven's sake—so no, of course I'm not. Are you?'

Dan very nearly laughed. 'Are you trying to be insulting?'

'No more than you were.' Megan gave him a serene look. 'Strange, isn't it, Dan, that even in this day and age you should be insulted by a question you were quite happy to ask me? And that's equality, is it?'

He gave her a long, considering look and the ghost of a smile hovered briefly on his lips. 'If it's equality you're after, maybe we should have thrown a coin to see who got first bath. Maybe even shared...' He gave a slow smile as he picked up his soap-bag. 'Don't you think?' But he didn't bother waiting for a reply—he needed to get out of there. And fast.

He took himself off to the bathroom and found himself furiously wondering whether she had had many lovers. Then told himself it was none of his business.

Unfortunately, his mother still hadn't succumbed to the temptation of installing a shower so, in order not to compromise himself completely, he did the next best thing and took the first cold bath he'd had since leaving boarding-school.

His skin was still all tingly as he wandered back to the bedroom to find that she had doused the lights, and he couldn't decide whether he should be grateful or sorry that the room now lay shrouded in darkness.

He closed the door softly shut behind him, standing very still for a moment until his eyes accustomed themselves to the gloom. He tiptoed over to the four-poster, where, through the lavish, richly embroidered hangings, he could make out the supine shape of Megan.

She was, he noted wryly, firmly tucked up beneath the silk coverlet. He could just see her nose above the crisp defining line of the sheet. She looked all sweet and clean and vulnerable and he felt that same dull ache as he grabbed a couple of blankets and quietly slid onto the bed next to her.

Megan felt the bed dip as it took his weight and tried to breathe normally, whatever normally was. She forced herself to concentrate on long, deep inhalations through the nose. Then she made a sort of snuffly, little groaning noise and flapped her hands around for good measure as she shifted onto her back.

'It's okay. I know you're not asleep,' said an amused voice on the pillow next to hers and Megan changed her mind about unpacking being intimate. Because it was pretty intimate to feel Dan's breath floating the short distance between them to warm the curve of her jaw and cheek.

She stayed silent and unresponsive.

'Megan?'

'What is it?' She sat up and snapped on the lamp by the bed, only to discover that the blanket had slipped and she was being confronted by his naked torso.

'I thought I told you to wear something!' she fumed, blinking furiously against the light. 'How *dare* you come to bed stark naked like that?'

'Shh! You'll wake the whole house.' His eyes glinted as he twitched one corner of the blanket just enough to reveal that he had maintained his modesty—just—and was wearing a pair of purple silk boxer shorts which came to about a third of the way down his thighs. 'See?'

Megan quickly shut her eyes. Yes, she did. And unfortunately she had seen more than she needed to. Dan might have been covered up, but he wasn't really what she would call *decent*, since fine silk was not the best fabric to choose for camouflage purposes. And, while she was no innocent, she was certainly not experienced enough to be able to deal with the fact that—for whatever reason—Dan was now very turned on indeed.

So was that just reflex? Or was it her?

'Megan?'

She turned away from him, speaking half into her pillow so that her words were muffled. 'Don't ''Megan'' me, Dan! I'm not

Katrina, you know, who can be swayed by a single glint from those grey eyes of yours!'

Didn't he just know it!

Dan gave a smile as he pulled a blanket around him and waited for the long night ahead.

A touch as light as the wind—barely more than a whisper—but a touch all the same.

Megan stirred, her limbs heavy with sleep. Something drifted over her hair, and tapped into some erotic memory deep within her unconscious. Wriggling fitfully, she turned onto her side and reached her fingers out, where they met with warm, satin flesh. Her fingers flexed and then curled possessively and she laid her head to rest on something warm and beating.

Through the gloom of the night, Dan glanced down, entranced by the whiteness of her cheek against the pale tan of his chest, where it lay so softly against his beating heart. He saw the gleam of her lips as they parted in unconscious invitation towards him, and felt stricken by both desire and guilt.

This was all his fault.

He had woken to find that he had moved right up to her during the night—and that his fingers had somehow tangled themselves in the warm silk of her hair. Beneath the eau de nil bedcover, her body had begun to move restlessly towards him. And instead of moving over to the other side of the mattress he had let her come just as close as she wanted.

And it seemed she wanted to come very close indeed.

He had asked himself what harm it could do—especially since she was safe beneath the covers. It was only human comfort, after all. An animal response—seeking out contact and warmth in the dark loneliness of the night.

He even convinced himself that there was nothing sinister about the way she was clutching onto his bare shoulders like that. And certainly nothing wrong with the way she was resting her head on his chest, so that the fine silk of her hair was spread all over it, like a dark-sheened banner.

He had barely moved, save when he felt the first heavy throbbing of desire. And then he had been forced to shift his body fractionally, and slide one hair-roughened thigh protectively over the spot where the ache was gathering strength by the moment.

She hadn't woken. Not even when his pulse had begun to rocket out of control. And her head was still lying on his heart. Didn't the sudden rapid thundering register in her ears?

More to distract himself than anything, he reached down to smooth away the strand of hair which had somehow stuck to her lips, and the strand kind of wound itself around his finger. And before he knew it he was letting that glorious tumble spill like honey over his hands again.

She gave a muffled little moan and he watched the undulation of her body as it moved beneath the coverlet.

He knew he should stop. Push her away. Or at least wake her...

'Megan?' he whispered.

Through the sweetest dream she'd ever been visited by, Megan heard a low, deep voice which made her melt inside. She moved her head by a fraction and her lips brushed against hair-roughened satin. Warm and living—musky and evocative—she could hear the muffled roar of a heartbeat.

She lifted her head up in confusion just as Dan gave in to temptation, and lowered his mouth to kiss her.

Wakefulness broke in at the moment his lips first brushed against hers and Megan immediately remembered where she was—and just who she was with.

Time enough to stop him.

But the night cloaked her with protection as well as robbing her of reason, and she didn't stop him at all. Instead, she found herself eagerly reaching her arms up to twine them round his neck, pulling him closer. And closer still.

Dan groaned as he deepened the kiss, feeling the shape of her body muffled by sheets and blankets. He was itching to tear off all those damned covers which concealed her and longing to cover her with his body instead...

He felt the sudden wild bucking of desire and tore his mouth away from hers with an effort, his eyes gleaming at her through the dim light.

'This isn't going to work like this, is it?' He shuddered.

For a dizzy split second, she had trouble deciphering exactly what he meant. 'What isn't?' she questioned muzzily.

'Sharing a bed like this!' he grated, and leapt off the bed as if he had been burned. 'I must have needed my head examining to have agreed to it!'

Through half-closed eyes, she watched him grab an armful of blankets and carry them over to the chaise longue. 'I was only trying to make sure you got a decent night's sleep. It seemed to make sense at the time.'

'Sense?' He flung himself down and felt the unwelcome resistance of a piece of furniture which was not properly sprung. 'About as much sense as agreeing to this whole idea in the first place!' he groaned, thinking that he seemed to be adding to the complications in his life, rather than removing them. 'Roll on Sunday afternoon,' he moaned, and shut his eyes with little hope of getting off to sleep.

CHAPTER SIX

MEGAN lay wide-eyed and sleepless for what seemed like hours, listening to the sound of Dan breathing over by the window and wondering if he was faking it, as she had tried to fake it earlier.

She tried the usual distraction devices such as counting sheep; then, when that didn't work, she counted backwards from one thousand. And somewhere around the two hundred and forty mark she drifted off into some kind of uneasy sleep.

When she woke, the room was still quite dark, but maybe that was because the heavy-duty velvet curtains were doing such a good job of keeping out the daylight. But when she glanced down at her watch she was astonished to see that it was past ten o'clock.

She rubbed her eyes with the back of her hands and pushed the covers back, watching Dan as she did so, but he did not even stir.

Moving very carefully, so as not to waken him, she walked over to the chaise longue.

He was lying on his side, his ruffled dark head pillowed on one of his hands, his long lashes making two ebony fringes which shadowed his cheeks. His face in repose looked younger. Softer, too. Sweet and sexy and kissable.

The blanket had slipped down to lie in folds around his waist, leaving his torso completely bare, and, for the first time, Megan could see what a magnificent body he kept hidden beneath his office suits.

The shoulders were broad and the chest solid enough to want to rest your head on. She bit her lip as she remembered that, during the night, she *had*.

He didn't have the great, bulging biceps of the gym fanatic, but he obviously wasn't a couch potato either—you could tell that from the honed muscle which lay beneath the softly gleaming flesh. His skin was the pale, creamy colour of fudge, with just a sprinkling of dark chest hair which tapered down into a mesmerising and provocative dark line towards…

'Seen enough?' came a mocking murmur, and the curtain of dark lashes were parted to reveal a pair of alert and very interested grey eyes.

'That wasn't fair!' she exclaimed. 'I thought you were asleep!'

'I know you did.' He yawned, and was about to turn on his back when he realised that maybe it wasn't such a good idea to put himself in such a vulnerable position... He stayed right where he was instead. 'I would have thought that, after what happened during the night, you'd have kept your distance.'

Megan wondered what was causing his eyes to darken like that. Surely it couldn't be the sight of her, in her demure white pyjamas, with her hair sticking out all over the place?

'What time is it?' he asked.

'Late. Gone ten. We've overslept.'

He groaned, and stretched. 'Black marks from Sally.'

'Who's Sally?'

'The cook—and housekeeper. Actually, more like one of the family. She served your dinner last night.'

'You didn't introduce me!' she accused.

'No, I didn't.' He completely forgot about positioning himself modestly and lay on his back and looked at her from between narrowed eyes. 'I had my mind on other things.'

Megan swallowed, wishing he wouldn't *do* that. Surely it wasn't necessary to their charade that he throw her the occasional glance which made him look as if he wanted to eat her alive? 'Do you think we should go down for a cup of coffee, at least?'

'Mmm,' he sighed, noncommittally. Frankly, it was the last thing he felt like doing. What he really wanted to do was to carry on where he had forced himself to stop last night. To pull Megan down on top of him, and kiss her a little and mess around a little and then...

He abruptly turned over onto his stomach, telling himself that it was simply proximity making him ache for a woman he did not normally find attractive. It must be. 'Do you want to get up first?' he asked. 'Or shall I?'

Megan was glad that he had turned over, because now he would not be a witness to the fact that she was blushing like a schoolgirl. And why? Surely she wasn't imagining that sensual undertone to his voice? She wasn't stupid. She certainly knew that he had been aroused last night—and she suspected it was the same right now.

But that was because men had bodies they couldn't always control. Bodies which were designed by nature to respond to simple sexual triggers—such as a woman of childbearing age sharing a bed with them! He probably would have reacted in the same way if she'd looked like the back end of a bus! And maybe she'd been stupid not to ask him to sleep on the chaise longue right from the start. He had certainly been expecting to.

'I'll use the bathroom first,' she said hurriedly, and grabbed Helen's idea of 'casual daywear', before rushing off to the bathroom.

After her bath, she put on the clashing pink pedal-pushers and a stretchy green top. She peered at her rear view in the mirror and shrugged. They would have to do.

She went back to the bedroom to discover that it was empty and that Dan had left a sheet of paper on the bed stating, 'Gone for a run—back soon, Dan.'

So should she wait or go down on her own? It would add credence to their 'romance' if she waited, but then she would

have to adopt all kinds of distraction tech-
niques while he was getting dressed...

So she wrote underneath his note, telling
him that she had gone in search of a cup of
coffee, and went downstairs.

She tried the dining room first but it was
empty and, on the way out, she bumped into
the woman who had served dinner the evening before. She frowned as she tried to remember the woman's name. Sally—that was
it!

'Good morning, Sally! I was...um...
looking for breakfast,' smiled Megan, feeling
slightly uncomfortable under the woman's
piercing stare.

'Breakfast is always served in the Garden
Room,' said Sally, implying that surely
everyone knew that! She gave a very deliberate look at her watch. 'And I'm usually
clearing the dishes away by now.'

Was it Megan's paranoia, or did Sally
wince very slightly at the pink glare from her
pedal-pushers?

'I know I'm late. We...I...overslept,' explained Megan apologetically, and saw
Sally's face tighten. 'Er, shall I eat now? Or

just have a cup of coffee and wait until Dan comes down?'

Megan saw a struggle going on in the woman's face while she clearly decided whether she was going to be helpful or not.

'If you're here as Mr Dan's partner, then you really ought to wait to eat with him.'

Megan nodded. *Mr* Dan—why, it made him sound about a hundred! 'Okay. Thanks very much.'

Sally looked as if she was about to burst with indignation. 'Of course, if his mother was here, there wouldn't be any of this sharing of rooms between unmarried—'

'Then we must thank fate for removing her for the weekend, mustn't we, Megan, darling?'

The deep, familiar voice was the most welcome sound that Megan had ever heard, even if the 'darling' bit was a little unnecessary. She turned her head and her mouth widened into a relieved smile. And a very genuine smile, she was surprised to note. 'Oh, Dan!' she said. 'You're here!'

Dan heard the anxiety which edged her voice, and an unexpected feeling of protectiveness washed over him. He glared at Sally, though not as much as he could have done. He knew that, to Sally, the rigid definitions of class were what made society work properly. He too had grown up under that system and he understood what motivated her behaviour, even if he didn't approve of it.

'I expect Sally's been helping you as much as possible, hasn't she, darling?'

'Oh, yes,' said Megan instantly. 'She has.'

Sally met Megan's eyes. And for a moment Megan thought she read a fleeting spark of thanks there. 'I'll go and make you both some coffee,' said Sally gruffly. 'And see if I can find you some pastries.'

Dan wondered why he still felt all keyed up and edgy—despite having run around the estate as if he were being chased by wolves. 'Was Sally okay to you?' he asked, once she had gone.

Megan smiled as they began to walk slowly through the open French windows of the dining room which led onto the terrace, where terracotta pots sizzled in the morning sunshine. 'Mostly. But she knows I'm a novice to all this. I guess I can't blame her for disapproving of me.'

Dan's face was thoughtful as they both sat down. 'I don't expect it's you she disapproves of. More the fact that I've actually brought a woman here and that I'm sleeping with her. She's probably feeling a little jealous—'

Images swam unwanted into her mind and Megan gripped the arms of her chair. 'Jealous?'

Dan's mouth hardened as he took in her expression. 'Oh, not in the traditional male-female sense. I haven't actually had an affair with Sally, if that's what you're thinking! She's a good decade older and she's married to the gardener. Or did you imagine I was happy to pounce on any woman with a pulse?'

'Stop putting words in my mouth, Dan!'

'I'm not. I'm reading them in your eyes,' he contradicted, but he saw the hurt which puckered her mouth up and relented. 'It's just that Sally has known me since I was a little boy—so she's more protective than your average housekeeper. She babysat for Adam and me—and she was always here waiting for us when we got home from school—'

'Where was your mother then?'

'Oh, she was far too busy with her charity work to pay much attention to her children. We were pretty much left to our own devices after my father died.' He gave a gentle smile in response to her tragic look. 'It wasn't *that* bad, Megan—it's just the way things were.'

'Didn't you mind?'

He looked at her, thinking that the outfit she was wearing today was even more bizarre than the yellow trousers. Bright pink trousers which came to only just below her knees and a dark green stretchy T-shirt were more than you needed first thing in the morning in the brilliant sunshine, when you weren't even wearing any sunglasses!

'It was the life I was born into,' he explained softly. 'The plus side was that in the holidays we used to run wild. Plenty of trees to climb and streams to swim in. And children can get used to anything.' He studied her eyes, which reflected the deep jade colour of her top. 'Like you did. It can't have been easy for you when your mother died. Especially not if you had to step into her shoes to look after your brothers.'

Megan crossed one blancmange-coloured leg over the other, realising as she did so that the pedal-pushers were at least half a size too tight and that if she didn't uncross them she risked splitting them! 'People always used to say how wonderful I was to cope, but it was a question of *having* to. If you don't cope, you go under. My father was always so busy on the farm, and I didn't want to see the family split up.' She wriggled her shoulders. 'So I guess it was purely selfish, really.'

Momentarily distracted by the movement of her breasts, Dan heard the clink of cups and looked up almost gratefully when he saw Sally walking towards them, carrying a tray. Hell, he'd never even *noticed* Megan's breasts before—she usually kept them hidden under loose grey or navy tops at the office. Now he was finding it difficult to tear his eyes away from them.

If it had been anyone else, he would have thought that they had been coming on to him, but he would wager almost anything he owned that she *wasn't*. Not Megan.

Sally put the tray down on the table.

'Thanks,' he said. He gave the housekeeper an unashamed look of appeal which had worked ever since he was a little boy, and which was rewarded by Sally giving

Megan something which approached a kind smile.

'Maybe she doesn't completely hate me after all,' observed Megan as they watched her go.

'Of course she doesn't hate you!' Dan murmured. 'She's probably just looking out for me. Maybe she's worried that you're going to break my heart into smithereens.'

'Oh, very likely!' She studied him, an irresistible desire to laugh tugging at the corners of her mouth. 'Still, if it's a risk you're prepared to take, Dan,' she mocked.

He held her gaze. 'Oh, I think so.'

He was playing games with her, that was all. Best not to react to them. Absently, she spooned double the usual amount of sugar into her coffee. 'What time is Jake due today?'

He noticed the faint flush to her cheeks. The way her breathing had become shallow. He wondered whether she would resist if he touched her. And found—extraordinarily—that he wanted to.

'Any time it suits him. Depends on his flight, or his whim. He's erratic—and unpredictable.'

'What else is he like?'

Dan smiled. 'He's a very funny and talented guy. And slightly eccentric. He was planning a career as an archaeologist until he was ''discovered'' while he was still at college. I think that maybe if he'd known what it was going to be like he'd have kept to his original plan. It's the fame thing. Some people love it. Jake finds it hard to cope with the lack of privacy, and people coming on to you for all the wrong reasons.'

Megan nodded. 'It must be terrible!'

He gave a wry smile. 'Well—there's terrible and terrible, Megan. I can think of worse jobs.'

'Yes, think of mine!'

'Very droll.' He sipped his coffee and continued to study her through eyes which were shielded by thick, dark lashes.

Megan looked around her with a slight sense of desperation. 'So what do we do today?'

'Whatever you like. You name it and it's probably here. Tennis. Swimming. Croquet—'

'I've never played before.'

'Haven't you?' He smiled as he lifted up the coffee pot to refill his cup. 'I could teach you, if you like.'

His expression made her heart race, but she didn't answer. Actually, she didn't trust herself to come over with just the right amount of take-it-or-leave-it interest. She surreptitiously ran her damp palms down over her thighs and looked instead at the way the lawn was so carefully mown so that it appeared all stripy as it stretched out into the distance.

Flowers seemed to grow and tumble everywhere; even the trees were threaded with climbing blooms of different colours. With the scent of the honeysuckle mingling with the scent of the coffee and the sunshine beating down on her face, she thought that she had never been anywhere quite so beautiful.

Dan watched while she closed her eyes, dreamily lifting her face towards the sun's heat, almost like a flower herself. Her hair gleamed in the bright light and he realised that it wasn't brown at all. More the colour of tea before you added the milk—with darker highlights of bronze, and spice. Leaning back in his chair, he sipped his coffee and enjoyed the quiet moment of peace.

'Hello, Dan!'

Megan's eyelashes drifted open and there was Katrina, wearing a cool cotton dress and looking as though she had been born just to stand around looking decorative on terraces!

'Katrina,' he nodded sociably, rising to his feet to offer her his seat. 'Going to join us for coffee?'

She smiled up into Dan's eyes, and slid into his chair. 'Thank you.'

'I'll go and fetch another cup,' he said.

The two women watched him go in silence and Megan wondered whether Dan had deliberately left them alone, realising that this would be the true test.

Could she convince the woman who believed herself to be in love with Dan that she was in love with him herself?

And how did she go about *that*? She didn't want to lie, or to rub the younger girl's nose in it. And neither did she want to be unkind, or to hurt Katrina any more than was necessary.

Megan thought about her third brother, who often used to get jealous of the baby— understandably he had blamed the infant for their mother's death. She'd had to deal with that, and she had gone about it by being calm and reasonable and by answering his questions head-on.

Katrina was sitting watching her, her big brown eyes lingering longest on the pink pedal-pushers, her pretty features creasing themselves into a tiny frown.

'So. I didn't really get a chance to talk to you much last night.' She gave a brief, perfunctory smile. 'Have you known Dan for very long?'

'No, not really. Just a few months.'

'A few months,' repeated Katrina disbelievingly. 'And is it true you work together?'

'Yes, we do. We spoke on the phone once; do you remember?'

'Vaguely!' Katrina bared her tiny white teeth like a kitten about to pounce on a moving ball of string. 'So how does it fit in?'

'What?'

Your *relationship*! Isn't it difficult to keep work and playtime separate?'

Megan thought about this trip so far. 'Amazingly enough, no,' she answered honestly. 'Not really. We're able to compartmentalise.'

'Lucky you.' Katrina stared at Megan's legs again. 'And does Dan like the way you dress?' she asked suddenly.

'Oh, he loves it!'

'Only—' Katrina caught at the strand of seed-pearls around her neck and twirled them around her forefinger and Megan realised that she was drawing her attention to the necklace which Dan must have bought her '—usually, he likes his women to be a little more... conservative, I guess.'

'And just how many of his women have you met?' asked Megan curiously.

'Oh, he usually keeps them hidden from *me*! He never brings them here.' Katrina gave a slow smile. 'I know what men are like—'

'Do you?' murmured Megan.

'Of course! I know that they have certain *desires*.' Katrina gave an apologetic little shrug. 'Desires they need to get right out of their system, before they settle down for good.'

Clever, thought Megan. Using that old 'nice girls don't' argument. And strongly suggesting just who Dan would be settling down with.

Katrina fingered her necklace again, and looked at Megan speculatively. 'Do you like my pearls?'

'They're very beautiful.'

'Dan bought them for me.'

'Yes, he told me.'

'He told you?'

'Of course he told me,' said Megan, very gently. 'I know how much he cares for you, Katrina—almost like a sister, in fact.'

There was a brief, painful silence, and for a moment Katrina screwed her face up, like a child about to cry. But then the moment was gone. 'You *do* know that Jake Haddon's arriving today?'

Megan nodded. 'I certainly do!'

'I don't know if Dan's mentioned it, but the last thing he wants is a lot of fuss,' said Katrina casually. 'You won't bother him for autographs or anything like that, will you, Megan?'

'I think I can just about manage not to slip into the role of pestering fan,' answered Megan wryly.

'Only I've known Jake since I was little,' said Katrina. 'His mother is a very good friend of Dan's mother—who is *my* godmother.' A pause. 'But of course—you haven't met her either, have you?'

'No, I haven't. The opportunity has never arisen before,' said Megan, perfectly truthfully.

'She's quite some woman!' purred Katrina. 'Quite old-fashioned, too. She likes tradition. And rules. In fact, Lady McKnight always says that in a chaotic society at least you know where you are with rules.'

Lady McKnight! Now why hadn't Dan bothered to mention that his mother had a title? Somehow Megan managed to prevent her face from reacting with panic. 'Any rules in particular?' she asked calmly.

Katrina glanced quickly across the terrace. 'Well, let me think of an example.' Tiny lines criss-crossed the smooth expanse of her forehead. 'Let's take marriage—'

Now there was a surprise! 'Mmm?'

'Marriage is difficult enough these days, wouldn't you say? Far too many divorces, and far too many people not even bothering to get married—you know what I mean, Megan?'

'Yes, I get the idea.'

'So if, statistically, the odds are that a marriage will fail, then the only way you can increase those odds is to level the playing field.'

'Oh? And how would you go about doing that?'

'Easy. The more a couple have in common at the outset, then the better their chances. And if you both share the same background, then it follows that you'll probably share a lot of the same interests, too. Makes life easier.'

'You've obviously given the subject a lot of thought,' observed Megan, with a small smile.

'Oh, I have!' Katrina's voice dropped to an intimate whisper. 'And I think Lady McKnight has, too! You see, people say that background doesn't matter these days—but it does. Of course it does! Oh, look! Here comes Dan!'

He had taken an awfully long time to find a coffee cup, thought Megan, wondering whether his lengthy absence had been deliberate. Had he wanted her to talk to Katrina— and, if so, then what had he expected the outcome of that talk to be? That, having spoken to her, Katrina would suddenly relinquish all claim on Dan out of a sense of sisterly solidarity?

Megan thought that if she *had* been serious about Dan McKnight, then Katrina would have certainly sown the seeds of doubt in her mind. And no doubt those seeds of doubt would have flourished into monstrously huge plants, kept alive by Katrina's obsession for Dan and Lady McKnight's apparent prejudice.

Dan walked over and looked down at Megan, a question in his eyes as if to say, Are you okay?

She supposed she was—if he considered it okay for her to be warned off in such an obvious way! But none of this was real, anyway, so why should it bother her?

Dan handed Katrina the coffee and sat down, and his eyes took on a bright, hard glitter as he observed the tension stiffening Megan's shoulders.

Very deliberately he reached out to where her hand gripped the side of her chair. Her fingers were cold and unresponsive and he covered them with his own, blanketing them with warmth and security.

And Megan realised that she felt safe and comforted by the protective gesture. In fact, she could have sat there quite happily all morning, with Dan holding her hand like that. And it was only when he took his hand away and she missed the contact of his warm skin that she realised something else, too.

That she was in danger of allowing herself to fall for Dan McKnight for real.

Unless, of course, she was very, very careful.

CHAPTER SEVEN

DAN insisted on showing Megan the estate, leaving Katrina sitting drinking her coffee, gazing moodily in their wake.

'Won't she mind?' asked Megan as they walked side by side over the small bridge which spanned the moat.

He was still angry on her behalf. 'Who cares if she minds?'

'Right,' said Megan slowly as she lengthened her stride to keep up with him.

The McKnight estate wasn't just big—it was *huge*. They walked for an hour in a big, looping circle which was like a small country!

'Does this *all* belong to you?' Megan puffed as they tramped alongside a stream which skirted a small wood.

'It's all family land—so no, not to me personally, nor even to Adam. We're only custodians for future generations. Everything— the house and the land and the farms—will be handed on down to our children.'

'If you ever have any,' she remarked.

He slowed his loping stride down. 'That's twice in the last twenty-four hours that you've made me aware of a biological clock I didn't even know was ticking. Or are you projecting your own desire for children onto *me*, Megan?'

Megan smiled. 'Maybe I am.'

Dan was taken aback by her answer. He had expected her to deny it, the way women always did. Mention love or marriage or babies and they always stared at you with feigned outrage—as if they'd never given a moment's thought to the most natural process in the world. He supposed they called it playing hard to get, but it had never worked on him.

He noticed that she hadn't lagged behind him at all during the long walk and glanced down at her feet. At least her shoes seemed quite sensible. Though quite why she'd decided to team sturdy brown brogues with those funny-looking trousers he wasn't sure. Still, it had certainly made the eyes of one of the tenant farmers stand out on stalks a couple of minutes ago! 'Like to sit down for a while?'

'Yes, please.' Megan sank down onto a daisy-strewn patch of grass and looked around her. In the distance she could see cattle happily chewing away at the cud and right then she felt just as contented as those cows did.

'Just how big *is* it?' she asked.

He raised his eyebrows mockingly.

'I meant the estate!' she enlarged furiously.

Dan smiled. 'Most people don't ask.'

'I bet they think it, though!'

'Probably.' He slid down on the grass next to her, thinking that her hair looked like a shiny mahogany curtain as the gentle breeze lifted it from her neck. 'I guess the house and land stand in about twenty acres. The farmland is nearly twenty thousand—and that provides most of the income from tenant farmers.'

Megan gulped. It made her own father's pig-farm seem positively tiny! She turned to him, and frowned. 'So why even bother going out to work?'

'Because if I didn't I'd be bored out of my mind.' Dan leaned back on his elbows and stared up at the inverted blue bowl of the sky.

'Anyway, most of the money is all tied up in a trust,' he explained. 'And I won't get any until...' Abruptly he turned over.

'Until?'

'Until I marry.' He shrugged.

'Must be a big incentive to tie the knot,' she observed.

'Oddly enough, it's quite the opposite. It has always felt like a noose hanging above my head.'

'What, marriage? Or the money?'

'Both, I guess. Wealth brings its own responsibilities. And, of course, with marriage there's always the question about whether the money is part of the attraction. Or whether you're loved just for yourself.'

Megan glanced over at him as he lay sprawled on the daisy-studded meadow. At his long, long legs. And the gauzy white shirt which might have been silk or might not, but whatever it was made of it was fine enough to show the tantalising outline of his torso, which she'd seen for herself in all its taut and hardened beauty. The wind had ruffled his hair so that it looked all untidy—so that, right then, he didn't look like Dan at all. Or, at least, not the Dan she was used to.

If he had thrown his stetson onto the grass and tethered his horse nearby, it would have... Megan sighed. It would have been a very realistic and sexy image. The aristocratic cowboy!

'Whether you're loved for yourself or not? Oh, come on, Dan—are you looking for compliments?' she asked him drily.

'Me?' He gave an idle smile as he watched a stray cloud scudding across the sky. 'What makes you say that?'

Megan picked a daisy and studied the circlet of white petals. 'I doubt whether money would be the sole attraction for a woman wanting to marry you. You're a very attractive man—as I'm sure you realised a long time ago!'

He turned onto his side to look at her, the lids of his eyes sliding down to half shield the glint of grey, but he was smiling. 'I *think* I'll take that as a compliment,' he mused. 'Even if you did sound as if you were having teeth pulled when you said it.'

Megan picked another daisy. 'And you could have *told* me that your mother was a Lady!'

The smile disappeared. 'Why should I?' he questioned coolly. 'Is it relevant?'

She registered the snub and glared at him. 'Only to the ambitious husband-seeker, I imagine.' She iced back a look cooler than his. 'Of which I am not one.'

'I wasn't suggesting for a moment that you were!'

She let that one go. 'It *is* relevant if you and I are supposed to be in love! Surely you might have told me something like that? As it was, I had to rely on Katrina to reveal that particular piece of information.'

He studied her expression. 'And was she foul to you?'

Megan shook her head. 'More condescending than foul. She tried to put me in my place—which is understandable, I suppose, under the circumstances.'

'That's very generous of you,' he said suddenly.

'Not really.' Megan sliced her thumbnail through one of the daisy stems and began to thread the tiny flowers together. 'She's still very young—'

'Only five-or-so years younger than you,' he pointed out.

'I know. She just seems younger.'

'Yes, I guess she does, though maybe it isn't surprising,' he agreed. 'She has had money virtually thrown at her since she was in the cradle.' He picked a daisy and handed it to her. 'Very different from your life, I imagine.'

Megan nodded and took the flower from him. 'And where's her mother now?'

'She has a flat in London. Katrina lives there with her. But her mother runs as wild as a teenager herself. I guess that's part of the problem.'

'She told me not to bother Jake Haddon. I think she imagined that I would go running up to him waving my autograph book in his face as soon as he arrives!'

'She had no right to say that,' he growled.

'Well, to be fair, Katrina doesn't really know me. She might very well have been saving me from making an appalling blunder in front of everyone, mightn't she? Especially if everyone else is behaving very matter-of-factly and not treating him any differently.'

'Do you always take the unbiased view, Megan?' he asked her solemnly. 'Or are you just trying to impress me? Because, if you are, I have to tell you you're succeeding!'

Megan laughed. The look in his eyes was very flattering, but she didn't really feel she'd earned it. 'I'm no saint, Dan!'

'No. I don't expect you are.' Suddenly his attention appeared to be caught by a movement behind her. 'Don't move,' he said softly. 'I can see something.'

'Is it Katrina?'

'I...think so.' He shifted his body so that he was closer and dropped his voice to a whisper. 'So how do you think we're doing so far—on convincing her we're lovers?'

'Lovers?' questioned Megan. 'Or in love? The two are very different.'

'Take your pick,' he murmured.

'Can she see us?'

'I'm not sure.' His voice deepened. 'Lean forward.'

'Why?'

'Just do it. At the moment our body language is pretty off-putting. We look more like combatants than lovers.' He touched her shoulder with the tips of his fingers and saw the slight shivering movement of her response. 'But this might help convince her

otherwise, don't you think?' And very gently
he pulled her down onto the grass beside him
and smoothed the hair away from her face.

He looked into her face for a long moment—with questions in his eyes which she
couldn't begin to understand. But who
needed understanding, when he had gathered
her this close in his arms? And who needed
explanations, when he blotted out the sun itself and began to kiss her?

'Dan—' she muffled helplessly against his
mouth.

'Shh!'

He kissed away her words and she let him.
Telling herself that this was a necessary part
of the act and she would just have to endure
it.

She was lying, of course. What did endur-
ance have to do with what was happening to
her? As soon as their lips touched she forgot
everything she had ever known—other than
how he tasted.

He tasted of toothpaste and he smelt of desire. Warm and musky and masculine and
sharp. In the night they had kissed through
the haze of sleep, but today everything was
crystal-clear.

'Dan!' This time she moaned his name with pleasure and the sound must have spurred him on. For as soon as he heard it he deepened the kiss, making a small exultant laugh as his fingers tangled in her hair.

'You're gorgeous,' he whispered.

'No, I'm not.'

'You damned well are!' Dan had to stop himself from cupping her breasts which were as soft as marshmallow. While, in contrast, the tips felt like tiny bullets, butting into his chest and firing straight at his heart. He could feel the cradle of her hips quite explicitly through the ridiculous skin-tight trousers and Dan felt himself grow hard, so hard he felt he might explode. For a moment, he honestly felt that if he closed his eyes and pushed against her he might...might...

With a groan he rolled off her and sat up.

Megan lay staring dazedly at the sky. That was a performance and a half. A command performance, she thought hazily. Her mouth felt bone-dry and her body was empty and aching. And she knew without looking in a mirror that her cheeks were all hot and flushed.

Now what?

She cleared her throat. 'Has she gone?'

Dan was sitting hunched up, his arms wrapped around his knees. He turned round at her question and Megan was startled by the dazed look in his eyes. A look she couldn't for the life of her work out.

'Who?'

'Katrina.'

'Katrina,' he repeated blankly.

'You saw her. Coming towards us. Remember?'

He narrowed his eyes to look into the distance, like a sailor squinting at the horizon, and Megan cottoned on immediately.

'She wasn't there, was she?' she said slowly.

He opened his mouth to deny the accusation, but then he remembered they'd agreed to be honest. And even if they hadn't he didn't want to lie to Megan.

'I can't be sure. It could have been a trick of the light.' He turned to look at her, and his grey eyes were assessing. 'But no, I don't think so.'

Megan stared at him. 'Then why? Why kiss me?'

He brushed a lock of hair back from her forehead and smiled the most enigmatic smile she had ever seen.

'Because I wanted to. I've been wanting to kiss you again ever since I held you in my arms during the night. And you looked like you wanted me to. Blame it on the birdsong. Or blame it on the sunshine, if you like.'

Blame? Megan nearly smiled. It was an odd word to use, under the circumstances. 'And once I've decided what to blame,' she queried quietly, 'what then?'

'Now that,' he said, and touched the tip of his finger briefly to her lips, 'is something I can't answer. Not when I'm this close to you and can't think straight.'

She gave a little smile, as if it didn't matter. And it didn't, she told herself. It didn't. Grown-ups were sometimes tempted to do things which made no sense at all—but it was only a big deal if you made it into one. 'Fair enough.' She shrugged.

Her easy acceptance seemed to bemuse him for a moment, until he scrambled to his feet and held out a hand to help her up. 'Come on,' he said. 'It's nearly lunchtime.'

They walked back towards the terrace to find the others sitting out in the sunshine, having drinks and waiting for lunch.

The colonel was draining a flute of champagne, while his wife sat beside him with a face like thunder. Neil, who was dressed for tennis, seemed pretty miserable, Megan thought. But his face lit up when he saw the two of them approaching.

Katrina looked beautiful but sulky, wearing a floaty floral dress and a great big picture hat, decked with flowers. With her hair loose and gleaming and hanging down her back, she looked as if she should be starring in a shampoo commercial.

So *had* she seen them after all? wondered Megan. Was that the reason for the big, long face? She was tempted to link her arm through Dan's, just to add credence to their togetherness, but something in the daunting set of his shoulders deterred her.

Dan held a chair out for Megan and then promptly sat at the opposite end of the table.

'Good morning, was it?' asked the colonel.

'Very pleasant,' answered Dan.

'Pleasant?' snorted the colonel as he leaned across the table to take the champagne

bottle out of the ice-bucket. 'I'm glad I'm not young again, if that's the adjective a man in his prime uses to describe a walk with a beautiful young woman!'

Megan went pink and quickly drank some champagne, wishing that she could disappear into thin air, like the genie in the lamp. She looked round. 'Where are Adam and Amanda?'

'They've driven out to the airport to collect Jake,' said Katrina, addressing her answer exclusively to Dan. 'His plane is due in at three, but you know Jake he'll probably want to do something completely crazy, like go via London! Or Scotland!'

Katrina took her hat off and flapped it around her face, looking extremely fetching as she did so. She sent Megan a sly look across the table. 'Oh, and your mother rang, Dan. I told her you were out and nobody knew where. And that you'd brought a girl-friend with you.'

'Did you?' said Dan evenly.

'Mmm. She seemed angry that you hadn't bothered to tell her.'

Dan gave an enigmatic smile but didn't answer, and Sally began to carry out large platters of food.

There were a few chaotic moments while room was made on the table. Megan felt baking hot as she tried to get enthusiastic over sweating slices of salami, and wished she had worn a hat, like Katrina.

She flapped a hand in front of her face and tried to catch Dan's attention, but he seemed to be resolutely refusing to meet her eyes. How contrary could you get? she thought. *His* kiss. *His* blame. *His* responsibility—and now he was acting as if it were all her fault!

Still. There was only one afternoon and one more night to get through. Tomorrow she could think about going home and then they would go back to work and it would all be forgotten.

As they had agreed.

So why did her heart sink at the thought of Dan going back to being Mr Cool?

Neil looked across the table at her. 'Fancy a game of tennis this afternoon, Megan? That's if Dan doesn't mind, of course.'

Megan paused long enough for Dan to be able to object if he wanted to. But he obviously didn't. 'I'm hopeless,' she smiled.

'How about a swim, then?'

'Lovely,' said Megan.

'How about you, Katrina? Going to have a swim?'

Megan felt quite sorry for the dismissive look which Katrina threw him, while completely ignoring his question. 'Dan, will you help me with my croquet shots?' she asked instead.

Megan held her breath as she saw him stare down into the perfect heart-shaped face, framed by the picture hat. Was that indecision she read on the aristocratic features?

'Not today, Katrina,' he said shortly. 'It's much too hot!'

Megan caught his eye at last. She was supposed to be his lover, and that gave her the right to ask him questions. She injected a honeyed note into her voice. 'And just what are you planning to do this afternoon, Dan, *sweetheart*?'

He knew what she was doing. Making the charade more convincing—that was all. Yet, infuriatingly, he felt the warm, hard rush of lust as her voice lingered over the term of endearment. He scowled.

He hadn't expected her to be this good an actress. And he knew something else, too. That if he was forced to watch her cavorting around the swimming pool all afternoon... He shook his head. That wasn't just *asking* for trouble—that would be like sending it a gilt-edged invitation!

'I thought I'd wander across and see one of the farmers.' His eyes flashed her a challenge. 'Want to come?'

Megan's responding smile was serene. 'No, thanks,' she murmured. 'I'm quite worn out after our long walk!'

CHAPTER EIGHT

AFTER lunch, Megan went upstairs and changed into her own swimsuit—not Helen's choice of a leopard-skin bikini, which consisted of little more than three triangles held together with bits of string! It was a plain navy blue one-piece, which was guaranteed not to offend or inflame anyone.

She went down and swam in the pool, with Neil ploughing stolidly through the water by her side. Ruth Maddison lay underneath a giant umbrella reading a magazine, and her husband snored loudly beside her. Katrina was nowhere to be seen and Adam and Amanda were apparently still *en route* collecting Jake.

After her swim, Megan fell asleep in the shade, and woke up to find that the sun had moved across the sky and that she must have been lying directly in its rays for the past—she glanced down at her watch—*hour and a half*!

It was getting on for five o'clock and everyone else had gone.

So why hadn't anyone tried to wake her?

Her face felt worryingly hot and she felt extremely sticky, and when she looked down at her arms and legs they were an unflattering lobster-pink. Great!

She jumped in the pool to cool off and swam several lengths mechanically then went back upstairs to her room.

Correction. *Their* room.

She opened the door quietly, but the room was empty, which meant that at least she could get ready in peace.

She padded along to the bathroom and wallowed in the huge tub until the water began to grow cool and milky-coloured and the afternoon sun had begun to dip in the sky. She slapped after-sun onto her skin, and was sitting in her kimono in front of the dressing table with a mascara wand in her hand when the door opened and in walked Dan, still wearing the jeans and gauzy shirt of earlier.

Their eyes connected in the reflection of the mirror.

'Oh, you're back,' said Megan automatically.

'I've been back for a while. I was just down by the pool, wondering where you were.'

'I fell asleep. When I woke, I thought I'd better get out of the sun. How was your farmer? Pleased to see you?'

He nodded. 'He's always pleased to see me. I've known him since I was a little boy. He taught me most of what I know about the countryside.'

He went over to stand by the window and Megan thought he seemed distracted.

'Megan?'

'Yes, Dan?'

He sighed as he turned round, and his eyes seemed troubled. 'Bringing you here seemed like an awfully good idea at the time—'

'It was never a good idea,' she realised aloud. 'Like you said last night, it was a stupid one.'

But he carried on as if she hadn't spoken, as if he was trying to work things out as he said them. 'And the main reason for that was because neither of us found the other sexually attractive.'

She put the mascara wand down. 'And you're saying that now we do?'

'You know damned well we do!' He stared at her. 'Didn't that kiss prove anything?'

'It was an enjoyable kiss,' she said carefully.

'Enjoyable? *Enjoyable?*' He laughed. 'So I'm to be damned with faint praise, am I?'

'I didn't realise that this was all to do with your ego, Dan!'

'It has nothing to *do* with my ego!'

'Then where exactly is this all leading?'

He glanced around the room as if he was looking for an escape route—like an animal which had suddenly found itself confined to a cage. 'That's just it—I don't *know*!' he snapped.

She raised her eyebrows. 'Why are you getting angry with me?'

'It was a crazy idea!' he raged, more passionately than she had ever heard him speak. 'I can't believe I even suggested something so fundamentally naive!'

'Well, maybe it wasn't so smart—but there's absolutely nothing we can do about it now. We'll just have to sit it out. And as pleasantly as possible,' she warned firmly, leaning forward to blot her lips with tissue paper. 'Has Jake arrived yet?'

'About an hour ago.'

'And did you get to talk to him?'

'Not much. He's jet-lagged. I wouldn't expect too much from him. If you're hoping for sparkling repartee, you could be heading for a disappointment. In fact, it wouldn't surprise me if he went straight to bed and decided to skip out on dinner altogether. And, for heaven's sake, don't look as if the bottom has fallen out of your world!

'I will be *very* disappointed,' she teased. 'You may consider yourself top dog, Dan, but if I've come all this way for nothing—' She shrugged, the movement causing the kimono to ruck over her breasts. 'Whatever will I say to my flatmate?'

On some kind of sensual auto-pilot, Dan felt his pupils darken in response, not just to her gesture, but to this newer, more assured Megan. And his heart began to pick up pace as he realised what was so different about her. Her eyes looked huge and sultry and her lips gleamed with a siren's promise. He felt the kick of desire as it blasted its way into his system again. 'Is that why you're wearing make-up?' he demanded. 'For Jake's benefit?'

'Oh, Dan!' she mocked, appalled by how much she liked that note of jealous possession. 'I may be a farmer's daughter, but even we country girls know that you don't go down to dinner looking like you've been out working in the fresh air all day!'

Pity, he thought automatically, his eyes drifting to the sombre black gown which was hanging at the front of the wardrobe.

'And is that what you're wearing?'

'Don't you like it?'

'It isn't in quite the same league as those yellow trousers. Or the pink things you were wearing today.' He chose his words carefully. 'You—er—certainly present a different image away from the office, Megan. I wasn't expecting you to be quite so…'

'So?'

'Flamboyant,' he finished.

He was so far off the mark that she felt she had better enlighten him. 'I'm not usually. I borrowed those clothes.'

'You *borrowed* them?'

'Yes, I did. Don't look so shocked, Dan! Women often do borrow clothes.'

His eyes softened. There was something terribly touching about her openness. 'Why?'

'Because most of my clothes are dead ordinary. Nice enough, but not quite nice enough for flashy weekends in the country like these. Except that I didn't get it quite right, did I? They were too loud for daytime, and everyone looked down their noses at them.'

'Not everyone,' he contradicted. 'I thought the yellow trousers looked pretty good myself. A little unconventional, perhaps, but very flattering.' Though it might be best not to elaborate on how pert they made her bottom look, or how slinkily long her legs were in them. He had gone out this afternoon to try to work those particular demons out of his system. '*Very* flattering,' he finished on a sigh.

'Why, thank you, Dan!' Megan smiled at him in the mirror. His chin was slightly dark with faint shadow and the sunlight behind him illuminated the hard body beneath the filmy shirt. The four-poster bed made a perfect backdrop in all its green and golden glory. Too perfect...

Dan peered over her shoulder. Behind the black dress, he could see the tantalising glimpse of emerald silk.

'What's the green thing hanging up?'

'The "green thing", as you so nicely put it, is a dress—lent to me by the same person who loaned the yellow trousers. But it's everything a lady shouldn't wear—low-cut, and skin-tight and obvious—so I've decided against it.'

'Sounds perfect,' he murmured, against his better judgement.

'Are you joking?'

He shook his head. 'Not in the least. Why don't you put it on while I'm in the bath and I'll give you my—' he met her questioning look with a slow smile '—opinion?'

He made giving his 'opinion' sound like the most erotic act known to man. Or woman. Which presumably had been his intention. Megan tried not to be affected by it, but she just couldn't help herself.

'And what makes you think I'll listen to your—' she drew the word out in retaliation, long and low and provocative—it was funny how flirting sometimes came so naturally '—*opinion*?'

He couldn't stop himself. He reached forward and rubbed the tip of his finger against the tiny pulse which fluttered at the base of her neck, enormously pleased when it throbbed into even more frantic life. 'This does,' he said softly. 'Look. See how fast your heart beats.'

Something seemed to be affecting her ability to speak. 'I'm excited.' She swallowed.

'Yes, I can see that.' The finger gently teased at the soft skin. 'And what's the reason for this sudden excitement?'

She tried to convince herself. 'It's because Jake's arrived—and who said it was sudden?'

Dan smiled. He didn't believe her. This was all to do with him and her, not some actor she'd only ever seen on celluloid. He was tempted, oh, so tempted, to trickle the finger down to where her breast began to curve. To cup it and watch it swell and curve and peak into his hand. But he had never made a pass at a woman just to prove a point.

He grabbed his bathrobe instead. 'Why don't you try it on?' he suggested again. 'Just for fun.'

Fun? thought Megan, once he was safely out of the way and she'd eased the resisting zip all the way up. He should try squeezing himself into one of these garments and then see if it was fun!

The bodice was tightly boned and cleverly shaped to give her an hourglass figure. It skimmed inches off her waist and somehow managed to push up all the flesh on her breasts so that they spilled over the low-cut top.

The skirt of the dress, in contrast, was very plain. Cut on the bias, it clung where it touched—and it seemed to touch her quite a lot. Especially on the bottom. It was the kind of skirt which meant that you needed to skip pudding if you didn't want people asking when the baby was due. But that was fine. She didn't have much of a sweet tooth, anyway.

The green silk whispered as she turned around and in walked Dan, his hair still damp, the faint sheen of steam clinging to his skin. He was wearing the towelling robe and as he walked she could see the occasional glimpse of one very tanned leg.

Megan opened her mouth to say something and whatever she'd been about to say quickly flew out of her head.

Because knowing that he was completely naked beneath was making her heart pound as if it was fit to burst…

Dan shut the door and stood very still, finding it hard to believe that this woman in the evening dress was the same woman who sat opposite him each morning organising all his conference calls in her shapeless tops and nondescript trousers.

'Oh!' he breathed softly as he saw the erotic contrast of emerald silk against the rich cream curve of her breasts. She had piled her hair up on her head and fixed it with tiny black clips—some feathered, some plain and some glitzy. From her ears dropped some outrageous paste jewels—jet and pearl and diamond—their fake brightness making her skin seem awfully pure in comparison.

Megan felt herself impaled by his gaze. Something in his eyes was making her feel all woman. A suddenly nervous woman. 'Like it?' she asked, as casually as she could.

'Do I like it?' he repeated, and the redundant question threatened to catch in the back of his throat. 'Yes, Megan—if you were holding a vote, then I think you could safely put me down as a ''yes''.'

'And do you think it's…suitable?'

'Turn around.'

Slowly, she did as he asked.

Dan swallowed as he watched her bottom swing round. Sweet temptation! Were his eyes playing tricks on him or was there some kind of magic at work here? He'd always thought of Megan as averagely slim, with no idea that beneath the functional clothes she wore to work lurked a body which looked just made for a man to lose himself in. And on. And around.

Megan waited in vain for a compliment, while the silence grew and grew. 'Well?' She turned back to face him but her protest died on her lips when she saw the dark hunger which haunted his eyes.

His gaze locked onto hers. 'What, Megan?'

'You haven't told me what you think.'

'There's no need to—you can see my reaction for yourself.'

'Should I wear it?'

'Yes, I think you *should* wear it. Why not?' He gave a smile and, for the sake of his blood pressure, resisted the desire to move any closer. 'With Jake there, people will be expecting some kind of floor show. You can help provide it!'

'Doing what?'

'Doing nothing. Just standing there will be spectacle enough.' He gave a lazy smile. 'And there's something about the Cinderella effect which rather appeals to me!'

'Do I look that different?'

'You know you do.'

Yes. And maybe she should have changed into the black dress and played safe, but Megan knew she had no intention of doing that. Because tonight she didn't want to feel like the scrubbed and sensible country girl with the skinny legs. She wanted to play the siren, the temptress, the *femme fatale*!

'Turn around again,' he drawled.

'I thought you'd seen the back.'

She heard subdued laughter deepening his voice.

'I have. I wanted to protect your finer feelings while I get changed, that's all.'

Megan quickly turned round. And then listened as she heard the gliding of silk—his underpants?—and the light whisper of fine lawn—his shirt?—followed by the more substantial-sounding rustle—his *trousers*? She swallowed in an effort to ease her sandpaper throat. How much longer was he going to take?

'You can look now, Megan,' he murmured. 'I'm quite decent.'

Huh! As decent as a man *could* be when he was sitting on a four-poster bed pulling black silk socks over such long and beautiful feet!

'I'll just tie my bow tie, and then we'll go down for a drink before dinner.' He slipped on his shoes and rose to his feet. 'Unless, of course, you want to do it for me?'

'You've probably had more practice!' she answered sweetly, because knotting a man's tie for him meant getting a little closer than was wise and could be a bit of a giveaway if your hands were shaking!

They were the first down by the poolside, where lanterns glowed orange and yellow, tied into the trees with shiny green ribbons. The citrus lights sparkled back at them from the water and the pool itself looked positively decadent, with candles gleaming brightly around the edge.

Just by the French doors, a large table was laid for eight with silver and candles and china gleaming in the subdued lighting.

'Doesn't it look beautiful?' murmured Megan.

Dan watched her obvious enjoyment with unexpected pleasure. Not a jot of jaded cynicism there, he thought. He observed the way her mouth was curving into a glossy crimson bow. And she looked beautiful, too. He'd never seen her with bright lipstick on before. It looked completely alien on her mouth, yet it did something for her that just a few days ago he wouldn't have dreamed possible.

It made her look as sexy as hell.

'Shall we have a wander around before everyone arrives?' he suggested, then glanced up at the sound of approaching footsteps. 'Oh, look. Here comes Jake—'

Megan jumped as she saw a tall figure approaching. 'Help!' she whispered urgently. 'What am I going to say to him?'

'Relax. Stay calm. Just be yourself.'

'*How?*'

'Megan, he may be a famous actor, but he's no different from you or me.'

'Now, why are you hiding out here?' drawled an instantly recognisable voice, and, as Jake Haddon made his way across the lawn towards them, Megan was able to see for herself what the Hollywood film star looked like, close up.

She blinked in surprise, because he was nothing like she thought he would be. Very tall and very angular—he'd made absolutely no concession to fashion or to the occasion.

His baggy cord trousers were surely much too warm to wear on an evening like this, and his shirt was sticking out at the back. His hair was thick and very wayward but it was his eyes which captured you most. His eyes were simply amazing. Pale, bright blue—bluer than the bluest thing she'd ever seen.

He drew to a halt in front of them, and stared at Megan, frowning slightly as he looked at her. He seemed amused. 'Hello! Who are you?' His accent was cut-class English. Silky and soft. Almost shy.

'I'm Megan, and I'm a friend of Dan's,' she answered shyly.

'Well, Megan, friend-of-Dan's!' And he picked up her fingertips and kissed them. 'I'm absolutely delighted to meet you!'

Dan laughed as he watched Megan turn pink with pleasure. 'Good to see you, Jake! Glad you could fit us into your busy schedule!'

Jake gave a shrug and Megan watched him with fascination. He looked so like a little boy lost that she immediately wanted to rush off and cook him a square meal!

'Don't talk to me about schedules!' he sighed. 'I've just finished filming in Manhattan—and they're rushing me off to Sydney next week!' He looked around. 'What I need is a drink.'

'Then you shall have a drink,' said Dan firmly, and pointed to where a table had been laid up at the furthest corner of the poolside. 'Let's go and sit down over there, so we can talk in peace before the others arrive.'

He touched Jake's elbow and actually grabbed Megan by the hand. And she was so astonished at the sudden physical contact that she barely noticed he was leading her and *Jake Haddon*—imagine!—across to a table which had a bottle of champagne cooling in an ice-bucket, as if they were at a fancy ho-tel!

The three of them sat down and Dan poured them champagne, while Megan couldn't think of a single thing to say. But no one seemed to mind, least of all Jake, who extracted a long cigarette from a crumpled carton, lit it and began to breathe it in with an expression of bliss on his face.

'Thought you'd packed that in,' commented Dan wryly.

'Oh, Dan! What I don't need tonight is a conscience!'

Dan raised an ironic brow. 'Why, what are you planning to do tonight?'

Jake didn't answer, for he had turned his attention back to Megan.

'You aren't what I expected,' he said suddenly.

Megan looked at him. 'But you didn't know I was going to be here,' she objected. 'So how could you know what to expect?'

Jake glanced at Dan, then back at Megan. 'You're the first woman of Dan's I've ever met—'

'Oh, but I'm not—'

'You're not just anyone's woman, are you?' agreed Dan equably. 'That's right, my darling—show Jake your feisty independence! Though I think you'll find that he's into female equality just as much as you are.'

Megan shot him a look of frustration. 'How kind of you to finish my sentences for me, Dan!'

He sent her frustration soaring upwards with a sizzling look of his own. 'My pleasure!' he murmured mockingly, suddenly realising how much he was going to miss playing the part of her lover. He splayed a hand possessively over a silk-covered knee.

Jake raised his eyebrows. 'If you two are longing to be alone, I can always leave,' he drawled in amusement. 'Yes? No?'

'No,' said Megan firmly.

'So where did you meet?' Jake asked.

There was a pause.

'We...um...we work together,' admitted Dan reluctantly. 'Megan is my...'

Jake looked at him questioningly. 'Your what, Dan?'

Dan frowned. All the appropriate words made her sound so servile. And she wasn't. Not at all. 'She's my personal assistant.'

'Gosh!' Jake raised his eyebrows. 'How unlike you to have an office romance!'

Megan thought that, when put like that, it sounded so...mundane. It almost made her want to leap to the defence of their fictitious relationship! She opened her mouth and shut it again, trying to ignore the mischief in Dan's eyes.

'So what's he like to work for, Megan? Does he boss you around at work?'

'He tries.'

Dan laughed, but his eyes were soft with challenge. 'No, come on, Megan—just what *am* I like to work for?'

It was tempting.

She turned and addressed her remarks to Jake. 'I'm afraid he *can* be very difficult!'

'That doesn't sound like a joke,' observed Dan.

'It wasn't.'

'What else?' asked Jake.

'He's clever. Exacting. And—' She turned to look into Dan's eyes which were darkly luminous. And I think I'm falling in love with him.

'And?' prompted Dan quietly, intrigued by the sudden softening of her face.

'And I'd much rather talk about Jake, actually.' Because, bizarrely enough, that now seemed much less intimidating than confronting her true feelings about Dan. 'Except that I've never met anyone famous before—and I haven't a clue what to talk about!'

Jake gave a little yelp of laughter, and leaned forward. 'Just tell me you love this man—' he clapped his hand on his chest

'—with all of your heart, and that will do for now!'

Megan stiffened. Did it show in her face, then? Or was it merely coincidence that Jake had echoed her thoughts so uncannily?

But Dan saved her from having to reply by reaching his hand along the back of her chair and allowing it to rest it on her shoulder. The game the two of them had been playing had taken an unexpected turn. Jake's teasing question had changed things and suddenly it felt real. Inexplicably real. 'Don't quiz her any more. She's shy, Jake.' He gave her shoulder a gentle squeeze and Megan turned to look at him in surprise. 'Aren't you, Megan?'

How could she concentrate on the question when he was looking at her like *that*? It was an unfair advantage. 'S-sometimes,' she stumbled.

'So tell us all the gossip instead,' instructed Dan.

Jake lit another cigarette, and inhaled. *'We-ll…'* And he launched into the most devastating verbal assault on his latest female co-star.

Megan found it fascinating to listen to insider gossip, but she was more than a little distracted because Dan continued to massage her shoulders.

Some of the tension in her body slipped away, only to be replaced by another, different kind of tension. She felt the muscle sigh with pleasure as it relaxed against the insistent movement of his fingers and her skin began to tingle with expectation.

They sat and waited for the others while the moon rose huge and white in the sky, and Megan told them about growing up on a pigfarm—enormously pleased to discover that she could actually make a Hollywood actor *laugh*!

'So tell me again, *how* do you castrate a pig?' asked Jake, his face contorting into a hideous grimace.

Megan demonstrated with a thumb and forefinger. 'Like this. See. You squeeze very carefully, and—'

'Don't!' shuddered Dan. 'I feel quite ill at the thought of it.'

Megan looked at the two men sharing the bench with her. A world-famous film star and a member of the aristocracy! If only her brothers could see her now! Or Helen. In fact—anyone she knew would do!

But it was interesting that, of the two, it was Dan who had the most compelling sex appeal. She only knew Jake from the big screen, but in real life he didn't seem terribly different from how he was perceived by the general public. His appeal was of the little boy lost who needed mothering, who would bumble and fumble his way into bed and earn the lasting devotion of a woman who liked to be in the driving seat. Not her type at all.

But Dan...

Dan's appeal was more basic and more commanding. Instinct told her that—or maybe it came from observing pack behaviour down on the farm and recognising true virility when she saw it. But she knew one thing. That despite the cool, analytical mind and the relative burden of inherited wealth there was a powerful strength which surrounded him like an aura.

And that if a woman was selecting a hunter-gatherer to protect and cherish her and gather her food and keep her womb filled with babies, then Dan would be the man. He didn't need any of the trappings.

'Is something the matter, Megan?'

She looked up at the cool question and found herself imprisoned in a steely gaze.

'Er, oughtn't we to go and join the others?' she asked. 'They'll be out soon and we shouldn't keep Jake all to ourselves.'

Jake winked at Dan. 'Oooh—a social conscience! She has the makings of a wonderful hostess!'

The three of them walked back across the grass towards the pool, where the others had already started to arrive.

Amanda was placing bowls of olives and nuts around the place, while Adam opened champagne.

Charles appeared, looking hot and uncomfortable in a too tight starched collar—and his wife was wearing a burgundy silk dress which had obviously been bought before she'd put weight on. Neil seemed pale and anxious and slightly out of place as he stood picking absently from one of the bowls of olives. He appeared slightly apprehensive, too—as though he had no idea what the evening held in store for him.

Well, you and me both! thought Megan wryly.

Katrina was last down—making an entrance in kitten heels which matched her sugar-pink dress—and she squealed with delight and threw herself onto Jake's lap, sitting and playing with his hair, as a child would.

'Anyone else coming tonight?' asked Jake.

'No.' Dan shook his head. 'Just us. That's it, I'm afraid.'

'Oh, *bliss*!' sighed Jake. 'No strangers asking me predictable questions! No boring chat-up lines from hideous women! I can get as drunk as I like and be confident in the knowledge that nobody will ring up the tabloids!' And he removed Katrina from his lap and wandered off towards Adam and Amanda in search of more champagne.

'There can't be many places that he can relax,' said Megan suddenly.

'There aren't,' Dan agreed. 'It's weird if you go out with him. Normally there's a split second of silence followed by a buzz of intense interest whenever he walks into a room. People don't know what to do—so they either completely ignore him or slap him on the back in an overly familiar way, as if they've known him for years!'

Amanda came up to them, carrying a tray of champagne. 'Have one of these,' she said. 'I've sent Adam off to find some music and we've given Sally the night off. That way we can be as outrageous as we like!'

'Oh? Anything particular you have in mind?' smiled Dan, taking two glasses and handing one to Megan.

'Well, there's wine and music—and lots of delicious food. The entertainment part is up to you!' She looked round the garden and gave a sigh of pleasure. 'Let's hope the weather will be like this for the wedding.'

'It's soon, isn't it?' asked Megan.

Amanda nodded happily. 'Only two weeks away! And about time, too! Adam carries the family trait of dragging his feet to get to the altar!'

'McKnights just like to be certain,' Dan mocked.

'But it's customary to walk up the aisle before you reach retirement age, Dan!' teased Amanda, and turned to Megan. 'I hope you'll come to our wedding.'

'That's terribly sweet of you.' Megan looked at Dan, as if to say, Help!

'We haven't really discussed it yet,' said Dan, not quite meeting her eyes.

'Oh.' Amanda looked disappointed, but she had the sense not to pursue it. 'Well, I'm going to put a light under the korma now— Sally has left us some enormous pots of curry! And it sounds like Adam has got the music going.'

They watched her go in silence as a sultry saxophone note shivered across the night air.

And Megan wished that the weekend could go on. And on.

She risked a glance over her champagne glass to see that Dan's expression was a complex puzzle of shifting shadows and she wondered what was going on in that cool and clever mind of his.

Dan frowned, wondering just what he had started. He had expected to be climbing the walls with boredom and irritation by now, longing to be able to drop Megan at home and go back to their normal, working relationship.

What he had not expected was this ease and enjoyment in her company—accompanied by an overwhelming urge to feel her body close to his. He shook his head, more than a little angry with himself.

'Katrina doesn't look very happy,' Megan observed, trying to defuse some of the tension in the man standing beside her.

'Doesn't she?' Right then, Dan couldn't care less. He found that he couldn't stop looking at the lush green bodice of Megan's gown, at the way it stretched tautly over her breasts. Deepest emerald against the milky skin, and the colour was reflected back in her eyes, making them look even greener. She looked like some sleek and exotic cat. 'No, you're right,' he agreed unsteadily. 'She doesn't.'

'Maybe we could get her to develop a fixation with Jake instead?' she suggested. 'He's probably used to women falling in love with him.'

'Probably.' But Dan didn't appear to be listening. 'Look, do you want to dance?'

'Now? With you?'

His cool grey gaze mocked her nearly as much as it ruffled her feathers. 'Yes, now. With me.'

'But won't we look slightly ridiculous? Nobody else is dancing.'

'So what?' He gave a glimmer of a smile. 'We aren't breaking any laws, are we? Come on, Megan, live dangerously. Let's show them!'

At those three words Megan's heart sank and her foolish little fantasy evaporated. Of course he wasn't dancing with her because he found her irresistible—he was dancing with her because Katrina was watching them!

Well, Katrina would get her money's worth! Megan decided she would act the part of besotted lover with a vengeance! 'Okay,' she agreed, and slid towards him.

As he took her in his arms, Megan lazily curled her arms round his neck and clung on like a limpet and Dan felt the erotic sensation of their hips fusing. He felt the sudden jerk and tug of desire as she moved even closer to him, their bodies fitting together like spoons.

Somehow, he forced his hands to remain still, when really he wanted to trail them over every inch of her in a slow and erotic exploration. And they were tantalisingly close to where her bottom curved so lusciously. He sucked in a hot breath of desire.

Over his shoulder, Megan could see Katrina's white and disappointed face, and for a moment she felt almost sorry for her. But then she reminded herself that Katrina was wasting her life on a love for Dan which would never be returned, and Megan's guilt ebbed away just as her breasts began to flower into life against him.

They swayed together, locked in each other's arms, oblivious to the sights and sounds around them, and, when Jake tapped on Dan's shoulder, he and Megan both blinked at him, like people emerging from a long sleep.

'My turn, I think,' said Jake, smoothly elbowing Dan aside and taking Megan in his arms.

Dan felt oddly disorientated as she slipped away from him. 'I'll go and help Amanda with the food.'

Megan watched him go, thinking how ironic it was that she was dancing with an utter heartthrob—and all she could think of was that she would rather be with Dan! Across the candlelit terrace, she noticed the hostile glitter of Katrina's eyes and she was glad when Jake whirled her around, so that she could no longer see her.

All this is for Katrina's own good! thought Megan fiercely as the music sent out its soulful beat.

Dancing with Jake was mechanical. He made the same moves as Dan's, yet it felt completely different. Maybe it was because she was instinctively holding herself further away, instead of being drawn irresistibly into the circle of his arms. Or maybe it had something to do with the fact that, although Jake had obviously been trained in dance, he simply didn't move as well as Dan.

'So how long *exactly* have the two of you been an item?' asked Jake casually.

'Exactly?' she laughed, but kept her face shadowed. She liked Jake and didn't want to lie to him, but neither was it her place to expose her relationship with Dan as a sham.

'It's still all quite new,' she told him truthfully.

He twirled her round. 'So I take it you haven't met his mother yet?'

'Not yet.'

Jake chuckled. 'Now that's something I'd like to see.'

'Why what's she like?'

'Strong. Single-minded—a lot like Dan.' He paused. 'Of course, she's been wondering why it has taken so long for him to settle down, and—'

'And she'll be surprised at his choice?' put in Megan, completely forgetting that she wasn't Dan's choice at all. She was, she realised, in danger of getting completely carried away with her role.

'Like I said,' he smiled, 'you aren't what I expected.'

'Too common?'

'Too normal.'

'I don't know if I like the sound of that! Isn't normal very boring?'

'Boring? I don't think so.' Jake gave her an odd kind of smile. 'Normal means seeing what's real beneath the glitter. And Dan's never known normal—not really. Not the way most people do.'

'Oh,' she said thoughtfully, thinking that that was a different way of looking at it. 'And what about you?' she asked suddenly.

'What *about* me?'

'Are you going to carry on making films?'

He looked surprised. 'That's an unusual question.'

'You don't seem to be enjoying it very much.'

'No.' He gave a heavy sigh. 'I'm not. Actually, I have the opportunity to go back to college, and study archaeology. That's what I was doing when I was ''discovered''.'

'Dan told me.'

He smiled. 'And I'm tempted. Very tempted.' He paused. 'Do you think I'm completely mad?'

Megan thought about it for a moment. 'Does it have to be so all or nothing?' she asked.

'How do you mean?'

Megan shrugged. 'Well, going back to being a student when you're…how old?'

'Thirty-three.'

Megan nodded. Of course. Same age as Dan. 'Might be difficult and disruptive, given your level of fame. So why not combine your film-making experience with your love of the subject and make documentaries instead?' she suggested. 'Or is that too simple?'

Jake stopped dancing. 'Sometimes the simplest things are the very things which count,'

he said slowly. 'Come on. The food looks
ready and Dan's glaring at me—I'd better
give you back!'

Megan laughed. 'You make me sound like
a book you've borrowed from the library!'

She was relieved that dinner was a buffet
affair. She wasn't in the mood for polite conversation around a dining table—not with
Katrina continuing to send her dagger-looks.
The curry was laid out in the dining room for
everyone to help themselves and then take
outside to eat.

In fact, she had no appetite at all, but a
thirst which raged. It was a warm, balmy evening and, instead of sensibly sticking to water, Megan found the chilled champagne surprisingly moreish. She managed to put away
almost three glasses until things started to
blur a bit at the edges and she stopped.

She flopped down on a lounger next to
Amanda, who began chattering away happily
about her bridesmaids, not appearing to notice that Megan was just nodding solemnly at
all the appropriate places!

Close by, Jake and Adam were telling Dan
about the problems they were having with
their computers, while Dan made a poor at-

tempt at looking interested. Ruth was valiantly trying to persuade her husband to get up and dance, and of Katrina there was no sign at all.

'Who wants a swim?' called a wavery voice, and Megan snapped out of her muzzy thoughts to see Katrina poised on the very edge of the diving board, wearing... Megan gulped.

At first glance it appeared to be a bikini, but a closer examination showed that it was her underwear. A black, underwired bra which defined a magnificent cleavage—and a wispy lace thong which was completely seethrough—emphasising the dull blur of hair beneath.

Megan glanced over at Dan, to see whether he'd noticed.

He had.

His eyes were mesmerised with wide-eyed disbelief as he watched Katrina curl her pink-painted toes over the end of the board, and do a provocative little knee-bend which made her breasts wobble.

She dived into the pool, her legs slanting back, and the globes of her bottom looked shockingly white against the thin black string of the thong.

'Is she sober enough to swim?' Megan asked Amanda quickly.

'Not really,' answered Dan, who'd over-heard her. 'Night-time swimming and alcohol do not mix.' He raised his voice. 'Get out, Katrina! Now!'

A water-slicked head emerged dripping from the centre of the pool. 'Why don't you make me?' she taunted.

Megan saw Dan's mouth tighten.

'Are you going to get out of your own ac-cord?' he asked almost pleasantly. 'Or does one of us really have to come in and haul you out?'

Katrina started treading water and shot him a provocative look. 'Come in and get me!' she pouted, then squealed just before diving beneath the surface in a flurry of bubbles.

'Leave her,' shrugged Jake.

'She's as high as a kite. She could hit her head on the bottom if she keeps diving down like that.' Dan gave a click of irritation, then sighed. 'Someone go and make some coffee. I'll go and get changed into my trunks. Tell her that. Maybe the threat of someone diving in to unceremoniously haul her out might bring her to her senses.'

He disappeared into the house, while Katrina continued to dive to the bottom. Then, just as abruptly as she had jumped into the pool, she climbed out again, picking up her discarded almond-pink dress while her teeth chattered madly.

'It's f-freezing!' she shivered, frantically rubbing her hands up and down her goose-pimpled arms. 'Think I'll go in and find a sweater!'

'Hurry up, then,' said Amanda. 'I want my pudding!'

But Megan felt uneasy. No—*more* than uneasy.

Dan was in the house getting changed and a near-naked and lovesick Katrina was also inside. Wasn't that just a recipe for disaster?

She put her empty glass down beneath the lounger, telling herself not to be so foolish. What did she think was happening, for heaven's sake? That the besotted Katrina would take this opportunity to burst in on Dan just while he was sliding on his bathing trunks?

She tried to sound interested when Amanda got onto the subject of buttonholes, but she had to concentrate very hard to pay attention.

And suddenly there was an almighty crash and the shattering sound of something breaking and Katrina shrieking, *'Dan!'* with a kind of wild hysteria.

Everyone turned to look at Megan, but Adam had already leapt to his feet. 'I'll go—'

'No!' Feeling thoroughly sober now, Megan stood up and everyone looked at her. Only she knew the full and rather sad little story. Whatever was happening upstairs in that bedroom was not for general consumption. And not just for Katrina's sake—for everyone's sake. 'I'll go and see what's happened. If I need help, I'll call. Honestly.'

She hurried inside and took the stairs two at a time, her fingers skimming the beautiful bannister, instinct taking her straight to the room she shared with Dan.

She didn't knock or cough or warn them of her arrival, but flung the door wide open.

Just in time to see Katrina lying naked on the bed—with Dan standing beside her, wearing nothing but a pair of trousers and holding her damp underwear in his hand.

CHAPTER NINE

KATRINA looked straight at Megan, blind triumph sparking like a fever from her eyes. 'Stop it, Dan,' she said huskily. 'We have an audience.'

Dan's face was like stone. Hard and emotionless. 'Get dressed and get out, Katrina,' he said, his voice trembling with quiet distaste as he dropped her underwear onto the bed beside her. 'If you leave now, then there won't be a scene. If you try to make matters worse by staying or attempting to upset Megan any more than you already have done, then there will. I can assure you of that.'

'And wouldn't you just hate that?' sneered Katrina. 'What would it do for your purer-than-pure image if they knew that you'd dragged me in here to try to seduce me?'

Megan bit back her disgust, and Dan must have seen her, for his eyes darkened with concern.

'I think my patience may have just reached breaking point, Katrina,' he observed softly. 'So are you going or not?'

Making a choking noise at the back of her throat, Katrina grabbed hold of her discarded bra and panties, but didn't make any effort to put them on, or to cover up her magnificent breasts.

'Yes, I'm going!' she spat at him. She slithered off the bed, stepping over the pieces of shattered table-lamp which were lying on the floor, then turned to Megan. 'And don't think he wouldn't have had sex with me, if you hadn't walked in and disturbed us—because he would! Ask him if he was turned on. Go on, *ask* him! How does that make you feel, Megan?'

'It makes me feel sorry for you, Katrina, if you must know,' answered Megan quietly.

By the door, Katrina stopped and turned around. '*Sorry* for me?'

'Of course it does.' Megan sighed, every last bit of sympathy gone by now. She felt like giving the girl a good shake. 'You're a very beautiful young woman, but you're wasting your time. And your life. You're not stupid. You must *know* that Dan doesn't feel the same way about you by now. I just couldn't bear to humiliate myself like that.'

And Megan's quiet dignity seemed to work where all else had failed because Katrina stared at Dan, jamming her fingertips into her shuddering mouth as she read the emptiness in his eyes.

'You don't love me?' she whimpered.

Dan fought revulsion, telling himself that obsession could distort reality. 'You know in your heart that I've never loved you more than I would have loved a sister,' he told her. 'And you risk destroying even that if this continues.'

Katrina stared deep into his eyes, as if searching for the truth there. And she must have seen it, because her mouth crumpled like a pack of cards. She gave a strangled little cry as she hurled herself out of the bedroom, slamming the door shut behind her.

There was complete silence for a moment after she had gone, and then Dan said, 'Megan?'

But Megan shook her head as she stared down at the carpet. 'You don't have to say anything—'

'Oh, yes, I do!'

She lifted her head and her eyes were bright with furious tears. 'But why? Why go over it now? It was the most loathsome thing I've ever seen—and I don't particularly want to talk about it, if that's okay with you!'

Dan stilled, his analytical mind sifting her words and trying to make sense of them.

'Was it loathsome because it was so blatant? Or because it was unexpected?'

The truth came blurting out; sometimes you just couldn't stop it. 'No, you idiot! Because it was *you*!'

'And why should that bother you, Megan?'

'Oh!' She gave a frustrated little yelp. She wasn't going to shout it out in words of one syllable for him!

'Do you really think I was about to make love to her?'

'I only know what I saw,' she answered doggedly, although in her heart she knew the truth. 'And, like I said, it didn't make for very pleasant viewing.'

'She came in here while I was changing, stripped off and made a lunge at me. That's how the lamp got broken. When I told her to get out, she promptly flung her bra across the bedroom. The knickers followed.' Dan's face tightened. 'I was trying to get her to cover up and get out.'

'Well, you weren't making a very good job of it!'

He heard the trace of humour in her voice and felt relief seep back into his blood. 'You don't believe that I was about to have my wicked way with her?'

Megan laughed—a bizarre sound under the circumstances, but a welcome one. 'Oh, Dan,' she sighed. 'You mean, bring her up here and make love to her on our bed, knowing that anyone could walk in at any time because the door was unlocked? Come on! I really think you would have a little more finesse than that!'

Maybe it was the way Megan said *our* bed. Maybe it was that sweet, trusting look she was giving him. Or maybe it was the way the tips of her breasts had tightened into tiny, tight little buds that made him think that maybe she wanted him just as much as he wanted her. Dan felt his heart miss a beat.

'Do you?' he asked unsteadily.

'Of course I do! You aren't the kind of man who would take advantage of a woman's feelings.'

Dan scowled. He didn't want her making him out to be some sort of saint—not when he wasn't feeling in the least bit saint-like at this precise moment. 'How can you be so sure of that?' he demanded, and he could feel the blood in his veins begin its slow, relentless throb. 'When I want to…' he dipped his voice and smiled through it '…take advantage of you right now?'

Megan stared at him, emotion catching in her throat, hardly able to believe that this was Dan—*Dan*—saying something like that. But if she needed any further proof she had only to look into his eyes and see the truth there as clearly as the day itself.

He wanted her! It hadn't been her imagination or wishful thinking—he had wanted her ever since he had brought her here. *Just as she had wanted him.*

She frowned as she remembered his exact words. 'What, *now*?'

'Right now.'

'But people will be downstairs waiting—'

'So let them wait.'

'And wondering what has happened to us,' she pointed out.

'I don't think they'll be wondering for long—I think they'll have a pretty good idea what we're doing.'

Megan gulped, wishing he weren't so far away. The distance between them was making her feel as though this wasn't really happening and it was also making her feel nervous. But he wasn't a mind-reader.

'Well, don't just stand talking about it from over there, Dan,' she said softly. 'You could try coming over here instead.'

His eyes scorched her with their sizzling grey heat. 'One step further and I'm afraid I won't be responsible for my actions,' he warned.

She felt a great kick of excitement in her belly at around the same time that she became aware of the sweet aching in her breasts.

'Who asked you to be responsible?' she whispered back. 'I'm not looking for a moral guardian.'

In the fraction of the second it took for his clever, smoky eyes to narrow, Megan wondered if he was back to being Mr Cool.

'Lock the door,' he instructed huskily.

'Dan—'

'Just lock it,' he repeated.

Her hand was shaking as she turned the heavy old key and it creaked in the lock. 'Anything else you'd like me to do?' she questioned as she turned round and met his gaze full-on.

'Oh, plenty.' He smiled as saw the sudden wariness in her eyes. 'You've still got time to change your mind, you know, Megan.'

'It's not that. I just don't want you to think that I do this kind of thing—'

'All the time? I already know that. And neither do I,' he said softly. 'I just want you to be sure, that's all. Do you want me?'

'Oh, yes.'

'Then you've got me. End of discussion. Come here.' And he closed the distance between them and took her in his arms.

'Dan—'

'Don't you *ever* stop talking?' he interrupted tenderly, and tilted her chin upwards to make her lips more accessible, then parted their eager moistness with a lazy flick of his tongue. 'Oh, Megan,' he breathed.

She held onto him as his mouth explored hers with a thoroughness which sent her senses spinning out of control. She splayed her fingers greedily over his nipples, and he groaned her name in response, cupping her buttocks with greedy, attentive hands.

Without warning he brought her up hard against the cradle of his hips and she gasped aloud as she came into contact with the formidable power of him, squirming against him until he gasped too.

'Dan!'

This time he stopped kissing her long enough to ask the muffled question, 'What is it?'

She shook her head frustratedly, searching for the right words and realising that there *were* no right words. It had been so long...

For nearly two years she had been celibate—ever since she had split up with David, in fact. And David had worshipped her— courted her with slow persistence and an almost formal manner. But, even so, she couldn't ever remember feeling as she felt right now.

'I don't know if I can remember how to do this,' she said shakily.

He laughed. 'I'm a good teacher.'

'I'll bet you are.'

He began to slide down the zip of her emerald-green dress. 'Want me to undress you?' he whispered. 'Or do you prefer to do it yourself?'

Which let her know just how experienced he was!

Megan felt a sudden pang of panic. She was no innocent, but there hadn't exactly been an encyclopaedic list of lovers. In fact, there had only ever been David. Was there some kind of pattern to modern-day seduction that nobody had ever taught her? 'You do it,' she said, murmuring against his neck so she couldn't see his face.

Dan found the switch perplexing. One minute she was up front and red-hot—while the next she was sweetly shy.

Why?

It wasn't because she was a virgin—she'd already told him that. So what was it? Because she worked for him? Because they saw each other every day? Was she thinking about what might happen once they were back in the confines of the office? His mouth flattened as he acknowledged the folly of what he was about to do—but by then the zip was all the way down and her dress had pooled around her ankles and it was too late.

Much too late.

'Let me look at you,' he said unsteadily.

Megan stood before him, aware of the picture she must present. Her underwear was nothing to write home about—but then she hadn't been planning for this to happen. Her new uplift bra was fine, but her peach-coloured panties didn't even match.

But somehow none of that mattered. Not when Dan was staring at her like that, with an expression of sheer pleasure on his face.

'My legs are too skinny,' she said.

'Why do you always put yourself down?' He dropped to his knees before her and took her ankle in his hand, running the side of his thumb gently along the instep, and she gave a little yelp of delight. Why had he ever thought she wore trousers to cover up her fat ankles? 'You have the most beautiful feet I've ever seen.'

'D-do I?'

'Mmm.' The thumb now seemed intent on climbing the faint curve of her calf and from there it found a home in the fleshy little pad behind the knee. The thumb licked and flicked and then began to travel up her thigh itself, stroking each stroke so agonisingly slowly that Megan thought she would *die* if he didn't touch her...

'There?' he questioned innocently, as if he'd been reading her mind, and his finger skimmed the moist silk of the peachy knickers.

'Oh, Dan!'

'Oh, Megan!' he mocked, and he began to slide the knickers down over her thighs, burying his face in the soft, dark fuzz of hair at their juncture.

It was such an intimate thing to do that Megan jerked with pleasure and shock at the sensation of his lips touching her there. 'Dan!' she whispered, instinctively swivelling her hips against him.

He almost lost it. 'Do you like that?'

'Too much,' she moaned.

'No. Not too much. Don't you know you can never have enough of a good thing?' But Dan saw her shivering. Come to think of it, he was pretty shaky himself, and he realised that he didn't want to play the teasing games of sexual prowess. He wanted to make good, old-fashioned love to her. To cover her with his body. To impale her. And fill her with his seed. Oh, God—no! He didn't want to do *that*! Condoms! Where the hell had he put his condoms?

'Come here,' he said thickly, and almost dragged her over to the bed.

The caveman tactics seemed so deliciously at odds with the sculpted and aristocratic face. Megan saw his grey eyes blazing like the sun as he laid her down on the silken eau-de-nil bedspread.

And then he stepped out of his trousers and boxer shorts and came to lie beside her, their unencumbered skin touching for the first time, and Dan felt an indescribable sense of freedom. To be naked with her and next to her.

'Come here.' He pulled her down on top of him to plunder her mouth of all its sweetness, slowly opening all her senses to him. And then, when the waiting had become too unbearable for either of them, he parted her thighs with the smile of a man who had discovered treasure and eased himself into her slick heat.

*   *   *

Megan opened her eyes to morning sunshine flooding in from the uncurtained windows and Dan propped up on his elbow, studying her face as though he were memorising it for an exam.

'Hello.' He smiled.

'Hello.' She gave a sleepy yawn, lazy and relaxed in the light of that look. No post-night embarrassment there, she thought contentedly. 'Have we missed breakfast?'

'No, but I'm planning to.' He lowered his head and kissed the tip of her nose. 'Unless you're desperately hungry?'

'Oh, desperately,' she agreed, looping her hands around his neck and brushing her lips against his. 'But not for food.'

'No.'

He made slow, deliberate love to her, drugging her with the soft white heat of pleasure, and, by the time they managed to get themselves bathed and dressed, it was nearly lunchtime.

Dan yawned, wishing her could take her straight back to bed, while Megan sat at the dressing table, wearing nothing but the yellow satin jeans and a rueful expression. 'I don't think I can face going down.'

'Of course you can,' he said softly, running his fingertips all the way down the line of her spine and watching her shiver in response. 'I don't think there'll be any more trouble from Katrina—you saw her face. Mission accomplished.'

'Mission accomplished,' she echoed thoughtfully. They'd done what they had set out to do. So was that *it*? 'I wasn't thinking just of Katrina,' she said. 'What about the others?'

'What about them?'

'Won't they—?'

'Judge you?'

'I guess.'

'Megan,' he said patiently. 'We have been sharing a room for two nights now and every single person in the house will have assumed that we were having sex. We weren't, but now we are. So what's different?'

Put like that, she wasn't sure and she didn't like to ask. The pact of honesty between them was okay up to a point—especially when it concerned facts. But feelings were different. And at this stage of a relationship—that was if it really *was* a relationship—you couldn't really start asking a man about how he *really* felt about you.

That tended to make them run screaming in the opposite direction!

She looked over to the window, where sunlight flooded into the room and illuminated the motes which danced frantically in the air. 'It looks hot. Don't you think?'

'Hmm?' he murmured distractedly. He reached down to fondle the curve of her bottom, then groaned, forcing himself to move his hand away. Too tempting. And he'd barely got a wink of sleep as it was. He hadn't been able to keep his hands off her all night, and he didn't know why that fact should cause a faint blot of concern.

Oh, yes, you do, taunted a voice in his head.

It's because she makes you feel different.

And because you've never had an affair with anyone at work.

Never made yourself vulnerable by bringing your personal life into the office.

'We'd better go down,' he said reluctantly. 'Before they send out a search party!'

Downstairs, Amanda and Adam were lying by the swimming pool. Neil was mechanically swimming up and down through the bright blue water and Charles and Ruth had gone for a walk before lunch.

'Where's Jake?' asked Dan.

'Sped off in a taxi about an hour ago, heading for London. Katrina persuaded him to take her with him.'

'Katrina's *gone*?' asked Dan.

'That's right. She mumbled some excuse about having double-booked. Didn't believe a word of it, of course,' said Amanda, motioning for Megan to lie down on the sun-lounger next to hers. 'So what happened last night? All three of you simply disappeared after we heard that crash. Or shouldn't I ask?'

Megan looked over to where Dan was just adding ice and mint to two tall glasses. From this objective distance, she could see the definition of hard muscle as it rippled beneath the lightly tanned skin.

Her eyes travelled down the dark line of hair as it tracked from his chest right down to the waistband of his swimming trunks. And she felt such a great kick of lust that it took a moment before she was sure of being able to speak coherently.

'There was a minor misunderstanding,' she said cautiously. 'Which now seems to have been resolved.'

Amanda gave a huge smile. 'Very loyal of you, Megan! And I really hope this means that Katrina will stop pining for Dan and following him around like a dog who has lost its master.'

Megan opened her eyes very wide. 'You mean you *knew* all along?'

'I suspected. Anyone with two eyes in their head could have seen that she had developed the most almighty crush on him. I don't know why he didn't tell her to push off ages ago.'

'He tried. But I don't think he wanted to hurt her.'

'That's Dan!' Amanda picked up a bottle of sun-lotion and tipped some onto the palm of her hand. 'Always the gentleman.'

Megan thought of the passionate man locked in her arms during the night, and just about hid a smile. *Always* the gentleman? She didn't think so!

'But, unfortunately, it seems he's doomed to spend his life hurting women!'

Behind her sunglasses, Megan's eyes widened. 'Oh?' she asked, with studied calm.

'Oh, not intentionally,' put in Amanda hastily. 'Nothing like that! But Adam says he seems to have an emotional cut-off point in his relationships. He severs the affair—and the women just can't seem to accept that.' Her smile was sunny and genuine. 'It's obviously different with you, of course—I mean, you're the first woman he's ever brought home. So you must be very special.'

Special?

If only you knew, thought Megan wryly. I was just the emotional decoy who provided a few extras on the night!

'Here's your drink, Megan,' came Dan's silky drawl as he handed her an ice-filled glass. And then he frowned. 'Are you okay? You've gone awfully pale.'

'Oh, I'm fine. Just a little tired,' said Megan and, behind the security of her sunglasses, she closed her eyes.

CHAPTER TEN

DAN and Megan drove out through the gates of Edgewood House and the world seemed to explode in a white-blue light—illuminating a cluster of men, all pointing cameras at the car and blocking the road ahead.

'What the—?' demanded Megan. She ducked down instinctively as Dan slowed down. One of the men took the opportunity to press his face right up close to the window, distorting his features into some kind of monster mask which leered in at her.

'It's the press!' Dan snapped, jamming the flat of his hand down on the horn, making them all jump comically out of the way. 'Sniffing around for Jake, I expect.'

'How did they know he was here?'

'Who knows? People follow him. Taxi drivers tip the papers off. He has to run the gauntlet of obsessive press interest wherever he goes. It's the price of fame.'

'Then it's too high!' said Megan fervently as the car gathered speed.

But the drive back to London was curiously flat.

Megan was tired, but felt too strung up to sleep and Dan seemed preoccupied. They'd gone up to their room to pack after lunch and had ended up having a bout of very basic sex on one of the velvet-covered chairs.

It had been fast and furious and gut-wrenchingly exciting with Megan straddling Dan in a way she had never tried before, and which she'd found unbearably exciting. But Dan had gone very quiet afterwards. And, in the flurry of trying to make herself look as if they *hadn't* been having sex, Megan hadn't had a chance to ask him why.

Or maybe it was more than that.

She didn't want to play the role of a carping and jealous new girlfriend by firing a succession of questions at him, but some of the things Amanda had innocently mentioned had left her feeling ridiculously insecure.

And wouldn't it be a little foolish if she and Dan had spent the whole time being honest with one another this weekend, except for the one time when it really counted?

So she waited until they were within five miles of her home before shooting him a side-glance. She wondered why she was feeling so nervous, when she had thrown off all her inhibitions so thoroughly during the night.

'Dan?'

Dan had been miles away. He hadn't given work a single thought all weekend, he realised. Not like him at all. And really rather disturbing.

Because neither had he thought through the consequences of what had happened between him and Megan—and common sense told him that this relationship was a no-no. He just hoped that Megan was sensible enough to realise that it had been a glorious one-off, generated by close proximity and a little too much to drink.

But something in the tone of her voice made him wary. 'Yes, Megan?'

She said exactly what was troubling her. 'Isn't it going to be a little...difficult...from now on?'

There was an odd sort of pause. 'Difficult?'

His voice was pleasant, but something about his manner caused the little hairs on the back of her neck to rise.

'You know.' She wriggled her shoulders impatiently. 'Things are bound to be different, aren't they?'

'How?'

Her pussy-footing came to an abrupt halt. Why was he wilfully pretending not to understand what she was getting at, when he was probably the most intelligent man she'd ever met?

'How do you think?' she demanded sarcastically. 'The fact that we've spent the last I don't know how many hours having non-stop sex might just have *some* influence over our working relationship, mightn't it?'

'Only if we let it.'

Megan nodded. 'So?'

'So we won't let it.'

Just like that, thought Megan, her heart sinking.

He turned the powerful silver car into her road and Megan was ashamed of herself for thinking how small the houses looked. Why, you could probably fit the entire street into a couple of the McKnight fields!

Nothing much happened in the suburbs on a Sunday evening—and even less where Megan lived. And any hope of slipping home discreetly was immediately forgotten because Dan's engine sounded like a particularly noisy space rocket, re-entering the earth's atmosphere. He pulled up outside her house, and the sitting-room curtain twitched.

'Oh, look,' he observed blandly. 'Your flatmate is obviously looking out for you!'

It might have been her heightened sense of emotion, but wasn't there something awfully *condescending* about the way he said it?

'Yes, that's Helen—would you like to meet her?'

Dan tried to glance at his watch without her seeing, but he saw from her furious face that she *had* seen. He sighed. This wasn't turning out as he had expected—but really, just what *had* he been expecting?

'I really do have to look at some work this evening.'

'Yes, of course you do!' Megan stared fixedly ahead. 'What's the matter, Dan—the house too humble for you, is it? I'm afraid that my flatmate may not be a member of the aristocracy but she's—'

'That's *enough*!' he snapped.

'I thought we agreed to be honest with one another?'

'Honest?' His mouth curled. 'That wasn't honesty—that was just plain insulting! How dare you imply that I'm some kind of snob, Megan, when I've never given you any cause to do so?'

'I—'

'People think that the title and the money don't matter!' he stormed. 'Well, they damned well do! Even people who profess not to care or be impressed start judging you by it! Just because I happen to be tired and I have to do some work tonight suddenly I'm accused of looking down my nose at your flatmate!'

'I think you've said quite enough!' said Megan furiously, and resisted kicking open the car door. 'Would you mind getting my bags out for me, please?'

'Of course.'

She fished around in her handbag while he placed the bags on the pavement, and when she found the keys she dropped them so that they clattered in a silver shoal on the pavement.

Dan bent to retrieve them, and when he handed them back she looked so sweet that he put his hands on her unresponsive shoulders.

'Megan—'

'What?'

'Don't sulk,' he sighed.

'I am *not sulking*!'

'Well, smile, then!'

'I don't feel like smiling!'

'Would this help?' he asked softly. And he leaned forward to plant the softest kiss on her lips, felt her tremble beneath it, and regretted his rash decision to go home to work tonight. 'Maybe I could come in for a little while, after all,' he murmured.

Megan froze. What, squeeze her into his busy schedule? Spare a few minutes for another bout of brief and energetic sex? Well, she had more dignity than *that*! 'Don't worry,' she said coolly. 'I think my flatmate might be a little offended if we went straight in and disappeared off to the bedroom!'

'That wasn't what I meant!' he growled.

'Wasn't it?' Megan felt the words being torn from her lips, even though she would have willingly left them unsaid. 'What did you mean, then—a cosy little tea party for the three of us? Maybe followed by a walk through the extensive grounds?'

'Right.' Dan's face tightened. 'You've made your feelings perfectly clear. You think I'm such a sex-mad snob? Well, fine. Let's go with our original plan, shall we, Megan?' He stared hard into her confused eyes. 'For the purposes of this weekend, we agreed to suspend the normal code of conduct between employer and employee—'

'Well, we certainly did *that*,' she said grimly.

'Which led to our being far more intimate than either of us had anticipated!'

Megan hoped that her dismay didn't show on her face. 'Yes, I suppose that's one way of looking at it.'

There was a pause as he looked straight into her eyes. 'But, in order to resume a normal working relationship—'

Megan looked back at him, sensing that she was about to hear something she didn't want to hear. 'Yes?'

'I think it would be appropriate if we went back to how it was before.'

Megan stared at him, not quite sure whether she had heard him correctly. 'Now let me get this straight. Just so that there can be no misunderstanding.' She drew a deep breath. 'You want things to go back to what they were before? To pretend that it never happened?'

He opened his mouth to speak but his attention was caught by another twitching of the curtain, only this time the flatmate was staring at the two of them quite blatantly.

Dan sighed.

He liked Megan. He liked her a lot. More, in fact, than he could remember liking any woman before. She could make him laugh and make him mad as hell—but she certainly wasn't ever *boring*.

He frowned. Maybe 'like' was the wrong label to use. It was a bland, meaningless word which didn't seem to take into account the fact that even now he was itching to free her body from those constricting clothes and lose himself in her sweet softness again.

Maybe lust would be a more accurate description of his feelings for her...

'Dan?'

Her voice sliced into his thoughts. 'What?'

Hoping that he would flatly deny it, Megan clipped the statement out. 'You want to forget this ever happened?'

Her matter-of-fact tone helped strengthen his resolve. For wasn't he in grave danger of forgetting Megan's primary function in his life? She was his assistant, first and foremost—a colleague he respected and whom he didn't want to lose—which was surely on the cards if the affair continued. And her position was far more vulnerable than his. Because, when push came to shove, an assistant was far more expendable than a director of the company.

And how could they possibly carry on sharing the same office when they split up— as split they inevitably would? After all, none of his previous relationships had captured his imagination enough for him to want to continue them long-term. Though he had to admit that Megan was nothing like the women he usually dated...

Even so.

He met the question in her eyes and forced himself to respond rationally.

'That's right,' he agreed equably. 'We forget it ever happened.' Somehow he produced a smile. 'So why don't you take the day off tomorrow to recover, Megan? And, when you come in on Tuesday, everything will have settled down.'

It very nearly killed her, but Megan waved him off with a determinedly bright smile fixed to her face. Then she went inside and burst into noisy tears, which was enough to bring Helen hurrying over from her position behind the curtain.

'He's gone!' Helen announced. 'He's just roared off in that silver car and virtually taken all the tread off his tyres!'

'I know he's gone!' Megan sniffed.

'Why are you crying?'

'Because…because…oh, *Helen*!' And she started sobbing.

Helen looked at Megan in alarm as she handed her a crumpled tissue. 'Tell!' she instructed.

Megan dabbed at her eyes. 'It turns out he's an Honourable something or other and his family own the most fabulous estate you've ever seen—'

'Yes, I can fully understand why you're crying!' quipped Helen sarcastically. 'He sounds like a real loser!'

'I didn't mean that!' sniffed Megan.

'Oh?' said Helen, suddenly serious. 'Then what did you mean? What happened with the obsessive girl? Was she convinced by you two pretending to be lovers?'

Megan nodded. 'Oh, yes. Only we took the pretence a little further than I anticipated, and I—'

Helen stared. 'Oh, Megan, you *didn't*?'

'Yes, I did! I slept with him and it was wonderful and now I don't know what to do!' And she burst into tears again.

'Just take it slowly,' said Helen, in alarm. 'What else *can* you do?'

'I blew it on the way home, I think.'

'How?'

Megan shrugged. 'I came over as petty and small-minded and jealous. I made out he was a snob—and if there's anyone less like a snob it's Dan!'

'Well, don't worry. Tell him all that to-morrow.'

'He's given me the day off tomorrow.'

'Well, Tuesday, then.'

'But he's said that he thinks we should go back to how it was—'

Helen frowned. 'Well, that's better still! So you play it cool.'

'But I don't want to play games with Dan—at least, not the ones that you're talking about.'

'It isn't playing games, Megan—it's called survival. You know how men can be frightened off if they think a woman is getting in too deep. Surprise him! He'll be expecting tantrums and recriminations—so don't give them to him. Act normally when you see him.'

'Normally?' Megan gave an uncertain smile. 'I think I've forgotten how.'

Megan quickly realised that you couldn't turn the clock back. And how could she go back to being something she didn't want to be?

For a start, she couldn't bring herself to dress in her usual uniform of trousers and top. Dan had woken something else, apart from her sexuality. He'd made her feel so much a woman—a *real* woman—that she thought it was about time she celebrated her feminine side for a change, instead of always playing the part of the eternal tomboy.

'Helen?' she called, from the bottom of the stairs early on Monday morning after a long, sleepless night. 'Are you flying today?'

'Roma on Tuesday!' Helen called back, in an Italian accent. 'Why?'

'I've got the day off today and—'

'You want to go shopping, right?'

Megan blinked. 'How on earth did you know that?'

Helen appeared, wearing a man's T-shirt. 'Feminine intuition,' she yawned. 'And yes, I'd love to come shopping with you!'

Dan was already seated at his desk when Megan arrived at the office on Tuesday morning. Yesterday, he'd spent a long, unproductive day at the office, staring fitfully into space, followed by a largely sleepless night.

He looked up when the office door clicked open and his mouth, which had started to say 'good morning' in a pleasant and neutral way, now froze into an expression of astonishment.

And irritation.

Megan was wearing a red skirt which fell to about halfway down her newly tanned thighs, and a tight-fitting black T-shirt which matched the black suede mules. Scarlet-painted toenails peeped out outrageously. Her hair, which was obviously newly washed, hung straight and loose down around her shoulders, and she was wearing make-up.

She *never* wore make-up to work!

She looked glossy-bright and vital. Dan shuddered. She also looked absolutely gorgeous.

'What the *hell* do you think you're playing at?' he demanded.

Megan assumed a pleasant smile. 'And a very good morning to *you* too, Dan! I'm very well, thank you—how are you?'

A pulse began to throb at his throat. 'Megan,' he said pleadingly.

'Yes, Dan? You'd like some coffee? I'll go and make you one—I could use one myself.'

Dan groaned as she wiggled her way out of the office. Was she trying to punish him for the way he had behaved in the car on Sunday night? Come to think of it, she hadn't behaved so well herself. Had she?

He sighed as she came bouncing back in, coffee steaming from two plastic cups.

He scowled at the cup, looking at it with fresh eyes. 'Isn't there any china in the whole damned building?'

Megan sat down in her chair and began to sip her own coffee, her eyes asking him a mocking question through the rising steam. 'You've never complained before.'

'No.' A list of about four hundred things to do lay on his desk untouched. And so did his coffee.

He spent the morning in a previously un-heard-of state of not being able to keep his mind on the job. He found that he couldn't tear his eyes away from the riveting spectacle of Megan's ankles neatly crossing and re-crossing over each other.

He glared at them.

Megan looked up around lunchtime. 'Is something the matter, Dan?'

'Why should there be?'

'Because you haven't done a stroke of work since I arrived this morning.'

'Think about it,' he said silkily. 'And then ask yourself whose fault *that* is!'

'I don't know what you're talking about.'

He towered to his feet, and suddenly his substantial desk did not look so substantial any more. 'Don't you?'

'No, I don't.'

'Well, I'll tell you exactly who is responsible for my inability to work,' he ground out menacingly. 'You are!'

'Me?' She kept her voice indignant.

'Coming in to work dressed like *that*!' His eyes devoured the luscious swell of her breasts.

'What's wrong with the way I'm dressed?'

'Everything!' he snarled as his gaze lingered on her flat belly and the sweet curve of her hips. He remembered just what they had been doing at the same time on Sunday and suddenly felt as if he might explode with need and desire and frustration. 'Nothing!' he added confusingly.

Megan nodded. 'So everything and nothing is the matter with me?'

He was standing over her desk now and there was a look of such dark and exciting menace on his face that Megan felt the tips of her breasts begin to prickle with desire.

And he must have seen it, too.

Because suddenly he was walking round to the other side of the desk and was hauling her to her feet in the way that men only did in films—the kind of films where the man hadn't seen a woman for about five years.

His face was dark and hungry and very, very aroused.

'Dan?'

'Dan!' he mocked, but he was so angry and so excited that he crushed his mouth down on hers and he could never remember kissing a woman with such fire and such passion before.

Megan's breasts started to grow unbearably heavy—even before he had started to touch them with greedy fingers which almost made her faint with pleasure. She opened her mouth to the sweet onslaught of his kiss and felt intense pleasure begin to flood her body. And she wondered where this was all going to end.

Well, actually she had a very good idea of where it was going to end, if one of them didn't bring a touch of sanity to the situation.

'Dan, *please*!'

'Oh, you don't have to beg me, Megan,' he murmured softly. 'I'm ready and more than willing.'

'D-Dan.' But what should have been a protest came out as a slurred incitement, especially when he lifted her skirt and laid a blatantly possessive palm over one cool inner thigh. Megan squirmed with pleasure.

'Like that?' he quizzed, and his eyes darkened as he saw her mouth open, and the tip of her tongue slick its way provocatively along the bottom lip. He rippled his thumb over the cool, smooth flesh of her leg and saw her eyes flutter helplessly to a close. 'Oh, yes—I can see that you *do* like it.'

In her fantasy, he unzipped himself and did it to her there and then. But surely fantasies didn't have such realistic sound effects?

Megan's eyes snapped open to discover that it wasn't fantasy at all. That Dan really was unzipping himself and laying her across the desk and...

'Dan!' she cried, through parched and excited lips, as countless pieces of paper showered onto the floor like confetti.

'I can see you're going to have to improve your lovemaking conversational skills, Megan. All you ever say is my name!'

His voice was exultant as he prepared to make his claim, and she could see the magnificent power of him, hard and silky, as he prepared to possess her. And Megan thought she truly would die if he didn't...

'Say my name,' he urged, reaching down to tug her panties down over her knees, aware of little else than a primitive and urgent need to possess her. 'Go on, say it *now*!'

She stumbled the single syllable aloud as he thrust into her, which was presumably what he had wanted all along. But if Dan was wild then Megan was suddenly even wilder and she clung to his neck as if she were drowning—each long, shuddering stroke made her wilder still.

David had been a safe lover. He'd never made love unless under the cover of bedclothes and the protection of darkness. Never in broad, bright daylight on the...the...

'Oh, Dan!' she sobbed as his rhythm increased. 'Please! Please! *Now!*'

He needed no second bidding as he felt her begin to convulse helplessly around him. And his own orgasm was like a lightning strike to the heart and body and soul. He cupped her buttocks with the palms of his hands and drove himself into her, deeper and deeper and deeper, until they both collapsed, sweat-sheened and exhausted, across her now chaotic desk.

And the telephone chose precisely that moment to ring.

CHAPTER ELEVEN

THE HOURS which followed were some of the most excruciatingly embarrassing that Megan could remember.

First there was the humiliation of having to climb down off the desk and readjust their clothing. Worse was to come. Megan wondered whether there was anything more designed to make you blush than having to hunt through a pile of papers for your panties.

And then have your boss dangle them at you across the desk from an impudent finger.

'Looking for *these*?'

'You seem to make a habit of finding women's underwear scattered around, don't you?' she snapped unforgivably.

'What are you talking about?'

'Katrina's *thong*!' she stormed. 'Remember?'

His lips went white. 'How dare you?'

'No, how dare *you*?'

And, just to add even more disruption, that furious rapping at the door began again.

'Megan? You in there?'

'Don't come in!' screeched Megan.

'Okay, okay—where's the fire? Just that there are some amazing flowers for you out here!'

But Megan barely took the words in. 'Leave them outside!' She could hear a muffled whispering from behind the door, and shuddered to think what they might be saying. And they hadn't even bothered to lock the door!

'Anyone could have walked right in!' she snapped at Dan.

Dan was still shaking his head in disbelief as he buckled his belt, wondering if he had completely taken leave of his senses. Had he really just had sex with Megan *on the office desk*?

'Don't I know it!' he snapped, and went back over to his computer, switching it off with the kind of dramatic gesture which was completely alien to his cool, analytical soul. But that was how she made him feel...*damn* her!

'I can't stay here, Megan.' He shook his head, as if anticipating her reaction. 'It's no good. I'll go along to one of the virtual desks and work from there. You know where to get me!'

Megan stared at him in dismay.

Softshare had plenty of 'virtual desks'— desks which didn't belong to anybody in particular, but where you could plug in your computer and log on to the company network and happily work away to your heart's content. But most of the directors, including Dan, liked having their own offices.

'But you've never bothered using a virtual desk before!' she protested.

He whirled round. 'So what's the alternative? That I stay around here and we act out every page of the Kama Sutra before going-home time?'

'Of course not,' she said stiffly.

'Okay.' In his eagerness to get out, he almost wrenched the door off its hinges—only to be confronted by an extravagant arrangement of flowers which someone had left on the floor outside. He bent down to take out the accompanying envelope which simply read, 'Megan', and frowned. 'Who the hell are these from?'

Megan neatly plucked the card from his fingers and picked up the bouquet, cradling the flowers protectively in her arms. 'Wouldn't you like to know?' she asked acidly, even though she didn't have a clue herself.

But at least, as a diversion therapy, they couldn't have come at a better time! And once Dan had gone she opened the envelope with trembling fingers. It was from Jake and said, 'Thanks for all your down-to-earth advice. I owe you. Love, Jake.'

The flowers were magnificent—blue and white like a summer sky and exquisitely scented—but Megan couldn't bring herself to get very enthusiastic about them. She put them on her desk more as an act of defiance, hoping that Dan would quiz her about them. But he didn't even return to the office that day, so she took them home and showed them to a highly impressed Helen instead.

'You get a bouquet from *Jake Haddon*—and you're *still* downhearted? I just don't understand you, Megan!'

'Join the club,' said Megan miserably.

The following day, Dan had to fly to Sweden for a two-day trip, and he and Megan had an awkward and frosty dialogue just before he left.

'I've booked your car for ten,' she told him, wondering if she was imagining his look of brittle tiredness.

'Thanks.'

'The tickets for your flight and your hotel voucher are all in this wallet.' She handed it to him, noticing that he maintained only the briefest eye contact and gingerly took the wallet from her as if it were contaminated.

'Thanks again.'

'I think that's everything.'

'Yes.' He sighed. 'Megan—'

'No, please,' she said icily as she anticipated the emotional post-mortem he was about to launch into. 'I'm certainly not after the sympathy vote!'

'We can't just carry on acting like nothing has happened.'

'But we *aren't*!' she said. 'Are we? We're working in separate offices now, and we barely exchange a word except when it's absolutely necessary—and when we do you could ice your drink with the atmosphere!'

Dan nodded. 'I know.' There was a long, uneasy pause. Removing Megan from his life had not been as simple as he had anticipated. He sighed. It was true that, physically, she was no longer around, but that didn't stop her presence hovering tantalisingly on the margins of his mind. He'd thought about it and thought about it, and come to the conclusion that maybe they *could* carry on seeing one another—but not unless their circumstances changed. He watched her face closely. 'Which is why I'm thinking of recommending you for promotion.'

Megan's heart froze. 'Pr-promotion?'

'That's right. The vice-president's assistant is going to live in France—leaving the position open for you. It's a great opportunity.'

Megan stared at him in disbelief, aware of a door clanging shut on her hopes and dreams. She'd known, deep down, that their 'relationship' probably wouldn't make it past the starting-post, but she'd thought that he respected her work enough not to boot her out so unceremoniously.

'Say something, Megan,' said Dan.

'Like *what*? Don't tell me that you're expecting me to thank you for rearranging my life without even bothering to consult me?

For sending me to work for a man I've barely exchanged two words with!'

'But Marty likes you, and he likes the way you work—'

'Oh, *does* he? Even though he would probably pass me by in the corridor without recognising me?' She stared at him with accusation spitting from her eyes. 'What *exactly* have you told him, Dan? To make him want to offer me the job without even interviewing me?'

Dan couldn't believe what she was implying. 'You think I told him about our... weekend fling?'

So *that* was how he defined it! Megan felt quite ill. '*Did* you?'

'Of course I didn't!'

'Or taking me without ceremony on the desk?'

Dan went white with rage. 'Why would I tell him a thing like *that*?'

'That male prowess thing? Boasting about where you've done it, and with whom?' Megan shrugged. 'Who knows what goes on in what passes for a brain in some members of the opposite sex?'

'You see?' said Dan, as if they had an un-
seen audience in the room with them. 'This
is what happens when you mix work and
play—the whole thing degenerates into
farce!'

'I wouldn't know!' stormed Megan, still
hurting more than she had thought it possible
to hurt. 'I've never done it before! Perhaps
it's one of your rites of passage—that after a
few months you have sex with your assistant
and then move them on!'

'I have *never*,' Dan roared, '*ever* had sex
with my assistant before—not on the desk or
anywhere else!'

'Oh, do keep your voice down, Dan!
Everyone in the other offices will hear you!'

He drew in a deep breath with difficulty.
'My last assistant was with me for four years,
I'll have you know!'

She ignored that. 'But the bottom line is
that I'm to have no say about my future em-
ployment with this company?'

'Megan—'

'No, Dan,' she said stubbornly. 'If whatever you've got to say is just an attempt to
sweeten the medicine—then I'm not interested!'

'So you don't want a transfer?'

She met his eyes with a long and chilly look. Anything would be better than seeing him every day—and reminding herself of just what she was missing. 'Actually, yes—I think I do.'

CHAPTER TWELVE

BY THE time Dan got back from Sweden, there had been some earnest personnel-shuffling going on at Softshare.

Megan was now assistant to the vice president—'*very* grand', as Helen remarked—and Megan found that she enjoyed working for Marty Shreve. The American vice-president was focussed, hard-working and had a dry sense of humour.

More importantly, he was a happily married man!

Meanwhile, Dan was using a replacement who had been sent over from the agency. And Megan had been delighted to discover that her successor, while apparently being incredibly efficient and a very nice person, was a fierce-looking woman in her mid-fifties.

'Serves him right!' she said to Helen.

'Aren't you being a little hard on him?'

Megan turned to her housemate. 'I can't believe I'm hearing this! Have you forgotten who I'm talking about? This is Dan McKnight, who used me and dumped me!'

Helen frowned. 'I thought he was simply doing what you both agreed at the outset—treating whatever happened that weekend in isolation to the rest of your lives.'

Megan glared. 'Are you defending him?'

Helen sighed. 'I'm not sure. Why don't you at least talk to him, Megan? That's twice he's rung here, now.'

'Because I don't want to talk to him!'

'Right,' nodded Helen. 'Does that at least mean you're going to start giving the occasional smile again?'

'Of course.' Megan curved her lips experimentally, but Helen grimaced.

'You look like you're auditioning for a job in the Chamber of Horrors!'

'Thanks,' said Megan curtly, and went off to answer the phone.

'Megan?'

The voice at the other end was deep and sexy and delicious, but Megan didn't feel even the slightest flutter of excitement. 'Hello, Jake.'

'Oh, dear! Bad as that, is it?'

She opened her mouth to brightly deny it, but her lip wobbled instead. And he had confided in her. 'Oh, Jake!'

'Is it Dan?'

'*Yes!* How did you guess?'

'I'm an actor,' he responded drily. 'I get paid to observe human behaviour. I could come round.' There was a frown in his voice. 'But if I risk it and I'm seen your life will never be the same again! You'll be plagued by the tabloids from now to Christendom.' There was a pause. 'Why don't you come to the wedding with me and take your mind off it?'

Megan blinked. 'Whose wedding?'

'Amanda and Adam's. Remember? It's this weekend.'

'No, I can't.'

'Why not?'

'Because I'm not invited.'

'Yes, you are! Amanda told me that she added your name to Dan's invitation. Didn't he tell you?'

'No,' said Megan grimly, conveniently choosing to disregard the fact that she'd refused his calls. 'He didn't.'

'Well, my invitation has just got "Jake Haddon and Partner"—so why don't you come and be my partner, Megan?'

Megan hesitated, telling herself that there were all kinds of reasons why she should dismiss the offer out of hand. But something stopped her and she couldn't quite work out what it was.

She was miserable. Let's face it—she'd been miserable ever since they'd returned from that bitter-sweet weekend. Maybe Dan had removed her name from the invitation in order to take someone else. Had she been replaced in his bed already? And if that was the case, then wouldn't it be better to know? And to show him that she had alternative partners herself?

'Okay, Jake,' she agreed slowly. 'I'll be your guest.'

She could hear laughter at the other end of the line.

'You make it sound like a spell in prison,' he commented drily.

'I didn't mean—'

'I know you didn't.' He gave an amused sigh. 'Don't worry, Megan. It will be wondrously good for my ego!'

'Jake—'

'I know, I know,' he sighed. 'You don't want me to tell Dan.'

'Don't tell anyone,' she said firmly. 'I'd like to see their first unprepared reaction.'

She'd just put the phone down when it rang again and the voice was also deep and rich and deliciously sexy. But this voice had not been professionally trained and this time her heart *did* give a flutter. More than a flutter—it nearly leapt out of her chest.

'Megan?'

Steady, steady, steady. 'Is that you, Dan?'

'Of *course* it's me!' he exploded, then drew a breath. He was going to stay calm. He was.

'How are you?' he asked silkily.

'I'm fine.'

'Good.' Dan felt a terrible urge to hurl the telephone through the window of his apartment and go over there in person, and…and… But a lifetime of conditioning was hard to break in a couple of weeks. 'You haven't been taking my calls.'

'No, that's right. I haven't.'

He almost smiled until he remembered the grim reality. She was *very* stubborn. 'I've been tied up with this damned wedding; I'm best man—'

'Was there a purpose behind this phone call, Dan?' she interrupted coolly. 'Or were you simply recounting all your diary details?'

He'd never felt so angry in his entire life. Or so turned on. 'Are you busy next Saturday?'

'I'm afraid I am.'

A black, murderous rage threatened to envelop him, until he remembered. It was none of his business where she was going—or whom she happened to be going there with. He drew a deep breath. 'What a pity,' he remarked, as if he were offering some throwaway comment about the weather.

'Yes, isn't it?'

'I was going to invite you to Adam and Amanda's wedding,' he said, and then, just so there should be no misunderstanding, added, 'Amanda particularly wanted you to come.'

Amanda wanted. Not Dan. Stupidly, Megan noted the quick pain to her heart and was glad that he couldn't see her face. But maybe she should be thanking him for his honesty. At least he hadn't lied and said that the day would be ruined unless she agreed to be his partner. 'Did she?' she questioned, quite calmly.

So should she tell him she was already going, or not? Or should she just turn up arm in arm with Jake and set a thousand tongues wagging? But if she told Dan she *was* going with someone else, then mightn't *he* bring along a partner, in retaliation, if nothing else? Although he might just have fixed himself up with a partner already.

Megan was torn. She didn't want to lie. Maybe she should just come clean and...

Dan's voice butted in and interrupted her thoughts. 'I'm sure that she and Adam would both have liked you to be there,' he said coolly. 'But never mind. Goodbye, Megan.'

'Goodbye,' she echoed, and put the phone down.

But at least the wedding gave her something to focus on. Something to look forward to. She wanted to look more magnificent than she'd ever looked in her life, and quickly realised that if she wanted to wear a classy kind of outfit which would make Dan drool, then she really was going to have to hire it.

Cobham was full of exclusive shops which provided just such a service and offered advice on colour and stylists. Megan found it slightly ironic to learn that the only colour she should *never* wear was yellow—but when she eventually emerged from one of the changing rooms even the hard-nosed sales assistant stared in astonishment.

'Well, I never!' she breathed. 'What a transformation!'

Megan looked in the full-length mirror and it took a couple of minutes before her eyes grew accustomed to the new her.

She hadn't even wanted to try the outfit on—which just went to show you that you could live for twenty-five years without knowing what suited you!

It was one of those dresses which looked nothing on the hanger—a simple, floor-length column of silvery-grey material. It wasn't until you put it on that you realised the fabric had been designed to cling and to dully reflect the light back. So that it achieved the impossible aim of managing to make her look both slim *and* curvy!

There was a diaphanous silver-grey wrap to go with it, and an outlandish silver-grey hat pierced by a dramatic black arrow. All in all, thought Megan, with a moment of intense satisfaction, it was just the kind of thing to wear if you were accompanying one of the most famous men in the world to a society wedding!

The marriage was due to take place at a church in Knightsbridge, and the reception at the West London home of Amanda's parents, and, an hour before the appointed time, a huge limousine with dark-tinted windows purred up outside Megan's house.

'He's here! He's here!' chanted Helen excitedly, from her customary curtain-twitching position. 'God—he's getting *out*! Megan, quick—he's coming to the front door!'

'Well, answer it, then!'

'I can't! I'd be too embarrassed—I'd melt in a pool at his feet!'

'Helen, if *I* can talk to him normally, I'm sure you can.'

Helen's look spoke volumes. 'That's different. You're in love with someone else, so of course Jake Haddon doesn't impress you. And the fact that he doesn't impress you is what interests *him*.' She sighed. 'Oh, why is life so complicated?'

'Go and answer the *door*!' said Megan, tucking a final strand of hair out of sight and thinking about what Helen had just said. About being in love with Dan.

She could deny it fiercely to herself—heaven only knew, she had tried. Or tell herself that she hadn't known him long enough and that it was only lust. Or infatuation. Or, or, or... But against all that lay a warm and painful certainty that this was it. The real thing. So what did she *do* about it?

Jake was dressed in a purple velvet frock coat and dark satin drain pipe trousers. 'Like it?' he asked, with lazy assurance.

'Love it,' sighed Helen.

'It's certainly different!' observed Megan, biting back a smile.

The church was an oasis of beauty and calm—surrounded by the busy city traffic. There was a buzz of excitement as she and Jake entered, and she heard the almost imperceptible question on everybody's lips: 'Who's *that* with Jake Haddon?'

And then her heart almost had an electrical failure because the groom and his best man arrived, walking right past where she and

Jake were sitting—towards the front of the church.

And the best man, of course, was Dan.

Almost as soon as he set foot inside the church Dan was alerted to her presence by a sixth sense he hadn't known he possessed. His eyes found their target instantly and it was as much as he could do not to simply stand and stare at her.

She looked, he thought without exaggeration, the most beautiful and best-dressed woman in the church—and there was some pretty tough competition.

He bit back the bitter bile of envy when he saw that she was sitting next to Jake. So this was the reason why she hadn't returned any of his calls, was it? Got her hooks into Pretty-Boy, had she? He fought the urge to go up to his old friend and kick him into kingdom come, reminding himself that he had a duty to Adam—both as his brother and as his best man.

Megan stared down at her shaking hands, wishing that the bride would hurry up and arrive, so that they could get on with the wedding—because it was sheer agony sitting here and wondering which of the stunning women in the church Dan might have brought as his partner.

Could it be that foxy little brunette in the second row, who had clearly never heard the rule about not showing too much flesh in a church? she wondered. Or maybe it was the ash-blonde with the cartwheel hat and such long legs that she simply had to be a model?

But then Amanda *did* arrive, shimmering in a mist of bridal finery, and she looked so luminously beautiful as she began to speak her vows that Megan found herself caught up in the emotion of the service. All the way through it, she sniffed into the handy-sized packet of tissues which Helen had thoughtfully stuffed into her bag, along with an urgent request to tell Jake Haddon that she was always available if ever he was short of a partner!

At last the organ swelled with the rousing notes of the 'Wedding March', and Megan kept her gaze fixed on the altar as the bridal party made their way slowly back down the aisle of the church, determined not to meet Dan's eyes. Not now. She didn't know what she would see in them—and she couldn't risk what effect it would have on her. Because weddings were emotional settings, true—but allowing a tear to decorously slide down your cheek was slightly different from bursting into howls of anguish!

As he approached, Dan willed her to look his way, but her stony profile remained stubbornly set as she stared straight ahead. And then Jake murmured something into her ear and she turned her head to respond, that soft, easy smile lightening her face, and Dan felt so choked with anger that he could barely breathe. Since when had Jake decided to start being part of a cosy twosome with Megan? And surely he knew enough women to find one of his *own*?

Outside the church, the wedding party began grouping for the traditional photos. Jake and Megan immediately got separated and then people began to cluster round the actor like flies so that she couldn't get near him. But at least it gave her the opportunity to peep over someone's shoulder to snatch an unobtrusive look at Dan.

Unlike Jake, Dan was in traditional morning suit—and the soft grey of the jacket and the dark pinstriped trousers made him look both terribly formal and terribly sexy. An older woman was staring at him as if she were in the process of witnessing a miracle, and another woman—younger—stopped in front of him and gestured to his buttonhole with a smile.

Jake freed himself from the hordes of admirers and came to stand beside her, seeing her eyes fixed miserably on Dan.

'What's this called, look but don't touch?' he asked quietly.

Megan turned to face him with a bright, determined smile. 'No, it's called look and realise what a lucky escape I've had!'

'Hmm!' Jake sounded unconvinced. 'The car's waiting outside—shall we drive to the reception?'

'But we're not supposed to get there before the bride and groom!'

'Then we'll ask the driver to take us on a scenic route!'

Megan might have been missing Dan with a pain which was almost physical—but being whisked around London in a luxury car with Jake Haddon certainly went some way towards easing the pain!

In frustration, Dan watched them go—not having the heart to disentangle the chubby

three-year-old hand of the youngest bridesmaid who had decided that when she 'growed
up' she wanted to marry him.

'Take my advice—opt for the single life,
kitten,' he told her with a grim smile as he
watched Megan's silvery-grey bottom disappearing into the back of the limousine.

The bridesmaid's mother overheard him
and followed the direction of his glance.

'Lucky girl,' she said, a little wistfully.
'There'll be a lot of broken hearts if news of
that gets out.'

'News of what?' Dan's mouth tightened
with rage and frustration at the woman's innocent expression. As if Jake *owned* Megan,
or something. Because if anyone was going
to possess that silver-hipped beauty it was
going to be him! 'They've attended a wedding together!' he snapped. 'Not just announced their engagement!'

'Okay,' said the woman uncertainly.
'Sorry!'

Jake asked the chauffeur to drive them
slowly around the park, and it wasn't until
they drew up outside Amanda's parents'
house that Megan started to get cold feet.

'Jake—I don't think I can face going in to the reception.'

'Why ever not?'

'There will be a receiving line, won't there?' She swallowed.

'Yes. So?'

So Dan would be standing in it, she thought, but didn't labour the point. Because if she'd thought she couldn't handle it, then she really shouldn't have agreed to come.

'Nothing,' she said weakly, and let him usher her into the hall.

'And I wouldn't worry about meeting Dan's mother, if I were you,' said Jake cheerfully. 'I think the two of you are really going to hit it off!'

Dan's *mother*!

Megan nearly turned tail and ran. She hadn't given that part of the equation a single thought. Of *course* his mother would be there—she was mother to the groom as well as the best man!

She started feeling dizzy as they joined the line, which was moving far too quickly for her liking.

'Lady McKnight—I'd like you to meet Megan Phillips,' Jake was saying smoothly, and Megan found herself standing in front of a tall, elegant woman dressed in coral-pink, whose familiar grey eyes were the same colour as her hair. For a minute she was so flummoxed that she very nearly curtseyed!

'I'm very p-pleased to meet you,' she stuttered, and had her hand taken and shaken very firmly.

Standing near to his mother, Dan heard the introduction and almost exploded with rage. Who the hell did Jake Haddon think he was—introducing Megan to *his* mother? He looked coldly at the actor's handsome face and felt his nails bite savagely into the palms of his hands. He wondered just what would happen if he hauled his oldest friend outside by the scruff of his neck, until Jake's next words stalled him. And he felt some of the unbearable frustration lifting.

'She's Dan's girlfriend,' Jake smiled. 'He brought her down to Edgewood a couple of weeks ago—'

'You'd hurt your foot,' put in Megan helpfully.

'Yes, I had!' Lady McKnight gave a rueful glance down at her right ankle, which Megan now noticed was encased in a plaster-cast.

'That'll teach me to play tennis with somebody half my age!' Her accent was cut-glass and slightly intimidating, but the smile in her eyes looked warm and genuine. 'How lovely to meet you, Megan. I've heard that you're quite perfect for my son.' She lowered her voice. 'I can't tell you what a relief it is to know that *both* my boys are well on the road to providing me with some grandchildren!'

Megan almost died with embarrassment. But now was neither the time nor the place to tell Lady McKnight that she had barely spoken to Dan since they'd got back. And that she was hardly going to be put in the prime position of bearing her son's children—when that same son couldn't even bear to be in the same room as her any more! 'It was a beautiful wedding,' she said sincerely.

She moved along the line and murmured something conventional and forgettable to Amanda and Adam as she kissed them each on the cheek, but Dan's tall, dark head kept invading her vision and her senses—so that she could barely think straight.

And suddenly she was looking up at him, and her heart seemed to suspend all movement as she acknowledged just how delectable he looked.

'What exactly did my mother say to you?' he demanded, in an undertone.

She wilfully pretended to misunderstand. 'We were discussing what a beautiful wedding it was.'

'That's not what I meant, and you know it!'

Primly, Megan shook her head. 'Oh, do try and stay calm, Dan—it'll make your best man duties much less arduous!'

Unable to decide whether he'd like to shake her or kiss her, or both, Dan dipped his head to speak close to her ear, momentarily bewitched by the faint drift of her scent. 'Listen to me, Megan. We have to—'

'Be grateful that it turned out to be such a beautiful day? I agree,' she smiled, with sunny insincerity, as she jerked her head away from the warm temptation of his breath. 'Lovely wedding, isn't it, Dan?' And she moved away with relief, aware of a pair of eyes burning a furious hole in her back.

She made her way out of the hall towards the specially erected marquee, where waitresses were circulating with champagne, and

Megan grabbed one with shaking fingers and downed it in one.

Closing her eyes, she leaned back against a pillar, thinking how ironic it was that Lady McKnight had not proved to be the snob of Katrina's description at all. In fact, she had been an absolute sweetie—and her easy acceptance of Megan as a prospective bride for her beloved son only made the reality of the situation all the more bitter.

Someone standing by the entrance of the marquee started beating out a hand-clap which was taken up by all the guests as the bride and groom were ushered in, followed by the rest of the receiving line.

And Megan knew that she had to get out of there before she overdosed on other people's happiness. Because women with long faces on the brink of tears had no place at a wedding reception. Putting her empty glass down on a nearby table and grabbing her handbag, she stumbled out of the marquee on legs which did not feel like her own.

Dan, who had been carrying his friend, the bridesmaid, on his shoulders, scanned the flower-filled tent for a sign of Megan, then frowned. Where the hell had she disappeared to? Carefully, he slid the bridesmaid to the ground and found her mother. He remembered how snappy he'd been with her earlier, and gave her a conciliatory smile.

'You didn't see the woman in the silver-grey dress anywhere, did you?' he asked her.

The woman glowed beneath the power of that smile. 'You mean Jake Haddon's girl-friend?'

Dan gritted his teeth. 'That's the one.'

'I saw her picking up her handbag just a minute ago. She's gone.'

'Gone?' Dan felt as though someone had just blasted a hole right through his solar plexus. 'Gone where?'

'I didn't ask,' replied the woman with dry amusement, to Dan's retreating back.

He felt like a man in a maze. Or in a nightmare. Everywhere he went, he was stopped by well-meaning people who wanted to talk to him, while he couldn't utter a word that made any sense to his own ears. Conversation was deadened by the roaring in his head and the ominous thundering of his heart. He found himself nodding to everyone who spoke to him like an obedient servant—so that by the time he got out of the marquee and into the gardens outside he felt as if the world was closing in on him.

In his befuddled state, the gardens confused him even more. There were lots of different 'rooms', which had obviously been created to provide interesting diversions to the eye—but damn all use to a man with a mission.

And Dan had never felt so purposeful in his entire life.

The pounding in his head increased as he skirted a tennis court, his eyes fruitlessly searching for her in the nearby kitchen garden, where the brambles glistened like bruises among the spiky leaves.

He came to the rose garden last of all, his senses momentarily soothed by the fragrant blur of velvety petals. And that was where he found her—sitting slumped on a wooden seat at the centre of an old-fashioned bower.

She stared up at him mulishly, her face registering nothing as he came bursting through the arch of blooms, like a wish come true.

Dan looked around. 'So where is he?'

She pretended ignorance. 'Who?'

'Who? *Who?*' His eyes darkened. 'Who the hell do you think?'

'I don't know, do I?' she bit back sarcastically. 'That's why I'm asking.'

'Jake, of course!'

Megan shrugged. 'I presume he's inside, surrounded by a crowd of not very subtle women, as he has been for most of the afternoon.'

Dan took a moment to gather his thoughts. Logic told him that her answer didn't sound like the answer of a woman who was consumed with love for the actor. But he had to know for sure. 'Are you and Jake an item?'

'An item?' Megan studied him. 'What exactly do you mean by that, Dan?'

'You know damned well what I mean!'

'Oh, no, I *don't*!' she retorted. 'Or at least I hope I don't!' She met his look of confusion with one of fury. 'An "item" implies that I'm having sex with Jake. Is that what you think?'

'Megan—'

'Do you think—do you *really think*—that I would have leapt straight from your bed into his? Do you?'

'No, of course I don't think that!'

'But there's no *of course* about it, is there?' she fumed. 'That's what your clumsy, insulting question implied, Dan! And anyway—' she drew a deep, shaking breath '—why should you care, even if I was?'

He didn't even stop to think about it. 'Because I love you.' The words he'd never said to any other woman just came tumbling out as though they were a part of him. Which in a way, he guessed, they were.

She hoped her face did not betray the wild see-sawing of hope and disbelief which were currently raging a battle inside her. 'Oh, really?'

Dan's eyes narrowed as he sensed that the fight was not yet over. 'Yes, really,' he said softly.

She looked at him. 'And that's it?'

He felt the first faint glimmer of a smile. 'You want more?'

'Of course I want more!' she stormed, blinking away furious tears. 'Why have you been ignoring me since we got back from Edgewood?'

And the angry question somehow answered all his hopes and fears more than the most passionate declaration might have done.

'I've been best man at my brother's wedding—do you have any idea of the amount of work involved in that?' he questioned. 'Anyway, I have *not* been ignoring you.'

Her face assumed a look of mock-concentration. 'No? Well, let's count the times you've contacted me—'

'I rang you—'

'*Three* times!'

'Twice you refused to speak to me, and on the third occasion you were as frosty as hell!'

'Hell isn't frosty,' she pointed out.

He ignored that. 'I came to your new office to take you to lunch on several occasions, but you were never there!'

That was because Marty had insisted she get out and get some colour into her cheeks at lunchtime. He'd been worried about her. 'You could have left a note!' she accused.

'And said what? That for the first time in my life I'd met a woman I wanted to marry, and I was handling it all wrong? I love you, Megan,' he said again. 'You and you and only you. Always you.'

'Oh, Dan,' she gulped, and this time she gave up on the tears as one began to slide its way slowly down her cheek. She opened her mouth to say his name again, but only an odd kind of squeaking swallow could be heard.

He walked over to where she sat, and looked down at her for a long moment, as if committing her tear-stained face to a back-up file in his memory. Then, very gently, he pulled her to her feet and tightly into his arms, until he felt the trembling within her subside.

He picked up her left hand and studied it, and nudged his thumb along the base of her ring finger. 'So do you love me too, Megan?'

'You know I do!'

'And are you going to marry me?'

'But I'm not a suitable bride!' she wailed dramatically. 'What on earth will your family say?'

'Was that a yes?'

'Of course it was a yes—you crazy, crazy man!'

The faintest frown appeared on his brow. 'There's just one thing I haven't told you, sweetheart.'

Megan looked at him with suspicious eyes. 'Sounds ominous.'

'Not really.' He hesitated. 'It's about the house—'

'Which house?'

'Edgewood House.'

'What about it?'

The frown deepened. 'What if I told you that I was going to inherit it one day?'

She forgot the fact that she had loved that house with a passion which seemed to go bone-deep. About the bricks which were the colour of raspberries and the moat which could reflect gold or silver, depending on whether you saw it by sunlight or moonlight. 'But you're the younger brother.'

'I know I am.'

'And you told me that Adam would in-herit—'

He shook his head. 'No, sweetheart. I told you that *traditionally* Adam would one day inherit, as the older son.' He shrugged his shoulders and grinned. 'I just come from an untraditional family! Adam gets the lion's share of income from the farms—and I get the house. And, as my wife, you'll one day become mistress of Edgewood.'

It took a few dazed moments before she could speak. 'And how come you didn't tell me any of this before, Dan McKnight?' she demanded. 'Was this some kind of test I had